Blotsvil

Mary Steele is one of Australia's top writers for children.
Born in Newcastle, New South Wales, and now living in
Melbourne, she was a children's librarian, tutor and
freelance writer before the publication of her first book,
Arkwright (Hyland House 1986), the hilarious and
touching tale of a giant anteater who makes Australia
home. *Arkwright* won the Children's Book Council Junior
Book of the Year Award in 1986, and was followed by the
equally acclaimed sequel, *Citizen Arkwright* (1990).

Other popular books by Mary Steele include her
distinctly Australian tale *Mallyroots' Pub at Misery Ponds*
(1988); her book of short stories, *A Bit of a Hitch and Other
Stories* (1995); her tale of country life for kids, *Tenterhooks*
(1997); and the story of her own childhood in Ballarat
during World War II, *Beside the Lake* (2000). *Featherbys* was
short-listed for the Children's Book Council Book of the
Year Award in 1994. All of Mary Steele's books are
published by Hyland House.

Blotsville

Mary Steele

HYLAND HOUSE

For Josephine Mary Kirkby

and in memory of Cocky (pink) and Stumpy (white)
who lived within our family at different times

———

Hyland House Publishing Pty Ltd
PO Box 122
Flemington, Victoria 3031

Copyright © illustrations Jiri Tibor Novak, text Mary Steele 2002

National Library of Australia
Cataloguing-in-publication data:

Steele, Mary, 1930- .
  Blotsville.

For children.
ISBN 1 86447 049 6.

1. Cities and towns - Growth - Juvenile fiction. 2.
Community life - Juvenile fiction. I. Title.

A823.3

Edited by Nan McNab
Illustrations, layout, cover and text design by Jiri Tibor Novak
Printed by McPherson's Printing Group, Victoria, Australia

Contents

Who's who in this story

Mrs Abigail Chattery – an old lady; first owner of Galahad
Mr Gladstone Chattery – her husband, who died
 before the story began
Aaron and Lottie Bitzer – joint owners of Bitzers' Pet Shop
Max and Pippi Bitzer – their children
Bentley Plank – a developer
Galahad – a galah, the son of Ma and Pa Galah

Sulf – a sulphur-crested cockatoo
Manager of the Dreamydays Rest Home – who
   probably had a real name but liked to be called Manager
Mr Bert Blunt – an old man, the first owner of Sulf
H. P. Burpwistle – Mayor of Blotsville (for a while)
Douglas – a retired guard dog
Mrs Gloria Gusto – the next Mayor of Blotsville
Gilbert Culvert – the Town Planner
Mr Moon – Manager of the Blotsville Bank
Mrs Moon – his wife
The O'Riley Gang – bank robbers:
   Wily O'Riley
   Luigi Lumpy
   Headlong Harry McSpurt
and …
all sorts of other people who live and work in Blotsville,
such as:
   news reporters, TV film crews, police officers, bank
   tellers, shoppers, town councillors, a headmaster, town
   band, bulldozer drivers, kids, elderly citizens, sausage
   sizzlers, a District Nurse and a switchboard operator.

Chapter 1

Galahs up a gum tree

Mrs Abigail Chattery was seventy-three years old and she lived alone. Her husband, Mr Gladstone Chattery, had died, leaving her with nobody to talk to.

Her cottage, named 'Chatterswood', had once sat all by itself in the countryside, among paddocks and bushland. The old wooden house had settled down into its rambling garden, and Mrs Chattery loved to hear the rain drumming on the iron roof and gurgling along the spoutings into the water tank. She liked to stand on her back verandah and stare across the yellow paddocks in the summer, watching the flocks of birds circle among the trees. But as the years went by, new suburban houses and streets had been creeping towards Chatterswood until they were now just down the road, slowly covering the paddocks. They spread like a rash.

'A blot on the landscape, that's what those places are!' Abigail Chattery said to herself. 'But *I* still have my gum trees. Goody gum trees!'

Mrs Chattery talked to herself all day long, because there was nobody else to talk to. While talking to herself, she tried out interesting phrases which she had read in books or newspapers, phrases like *a blot on the landscape*. Sometimes she would stand at her gate and stare at the new houses crawling closer and closer over the hill. 'Blots on the landscape, all of you,' she would shout, '*Blots!*' She meant the new houses gobbling up the ground, not the people who lived in them, for she knew they had to live somewhere.

She called the creeping suburb 'Blotsville' as a joke, but newcomers, hearing her and knowing she was the oldest inhabitant of the district, thought that Blotsville had always been its name, perhaps in memory of an early pioneer called Blot. The new town council wondered about putting up a statue of the mysterious Mr Blot, but Mrs Chattery, with a tiny twinkle, said he'd been before her time – she really knew nothing about him – so they gave up the idea.

Mrs Chattery's gum trees were very old, even older than her house. There were three of them left, two still green and one quite dead, with bare grey arms raised to the sky.

Quite often, Mrs Chattery stood under these trees and recited, very loudly,

> *I think that I shall never see*
> *A poem lovely as a tree!*

She remembered this rhyme from her school days, but she couldn't remember the rest of the poem, except for the last line, which went,

> *For only God can make a tree.*

That's quite right,' said Abigail Chattery. '*I* couldn't make a tree. I wouldn't get to first base, even if I tried.' This was another phrase she had read in a magazine. She liked the sound of *getting to first base* although she wasn't sure what it meant; so far she hadn't played baseball.

•••

While Mrs Chattery was in her backyard reciting *I think that I shall never see a poem lovely as a tree*, two pairs of bright button eyes were also surveying the three gum trees. Ma and Pa Galah were house-hunting and Mrs Chattery's gum trees, being easily the largest trees near Blotsville, had caught their eye. Ma Galah liked the look of the dead one.

'That one might do,' she said to her husband, in Ga-la-language. 'Are there any door holes?'

'Wait a jiffy, my sweet,' answered Pa Galah, 'and I'll check it out.' He flew up to the crown of the dead tree and swooped amongst the smooth grey boughs, before zooming back to the fence post on which Ma was perched.

She cocked her pale pink crest at him. 'Well?' she squawked.

'There's a hole in that big branch,' said Pa, 'and the bottom is flat, so the eggs won't roll away. Come on, Ma, no time to waste!'

The galahs' feathers glowed hot pink in the sunshine and Abigail Chattery watched as the birds soared up to the hole. With their strong, curved beaks they ripped and nibbled and poked about, until the opening was big enough for a front door and the bark had been cleaned away. Ma and Pa Galah took turns to squeeze inside the hollow branch and spring-clean. Bits of rotten wood and rubbish shot out. Then Pa Galah flew into the next gum tree and came back with a bunch of green leaves to start lining the inside of their new home.

'Oh, joy and rapture!' exclaimed Mrs Chattery, clutching her hands together in front of her. She was especially fond of galahs, for pink was her favourite colour. She wore a pink straw hat for gardening, and even her spectacle frames were pink. 'Oh, joy and rapture!' she repeated, doing a little jig.

'Hoo-ray, hoo-rah for the ga-la-lahs –
They're nesting in my tree!'

•••

Ma Galah laid five white eggs on the gumleaves and sat on them over the next few weeks to keep them warm. One egg was addled, but four squirming babies hatched out of the others and then Ma and Pa were flat out feeding their new family. Mrs Chattery watched as they flew in and out of the tree, bringing food, and she could hear the hungry babies squeaking inside their hollow branch.

'Babies,' she beamed. 'Always hungry!'

One baby was bigger than the rest. He had hatched first and he usually grabbed the best bits of dinner from his parents' beaks. When he was strong enough, he was the first of the four to wriggle over to the hole in the branch and to look out. His mother almost collided with him as she arrived home with another beakful of mush.

'Now, listen to me, young ga-largle,' she scolded, as soon as she had emptied her mushy mouthful into the babies' throats. 'You must not go near that hole until you are ready to fly, for more than likely you'll fall out, right down to the ground, *splat*, and that will be that. If you don't freeze to death, you'll make a juicy supper for some slithery snake or creepy cat.' Ma Galah was very wary of slithery, creepy creatures.

'It pays to listen to your mother,' nodded Pa Galah. 'She knows best, see?'

But the baby galah didn't believe them. He knew

nothing about snakes or cats. What he saw through the door hole was so exciting that he just *had* to look out. As soon as his parents had flown off again, he grabbed the edge of the hole with his little feet and perched on the rim, so that he could peer around still further. And then, of course, he *fell out.*

As she flew back towards the tree, his mother saw the tiny body plummeting down to the earth, its tiny wings waving uselessly. Down … down … down … SPLUDGE!

Ma opened her beak to screech and all the food fell out. 'You *stupid* galah!' she shrieked at him. 'You *dill*!'

Pa arrived and they both flapped round and round just above their baby, shouting at him in their Ga-la-language, things like, 'Why didn't you listen to your mother?' and '*Idiot*!' But there was no way they could get him back to his nest. They just had to leave him while they went back to feed the other three, who were all screaming for dinner. Ma and Pa had often lost adventurous babies in this way. 'They will not listen!' Ma said to Pa, every time it happened.

It was there on the ground that Mrs Chattery found the baby bird, lying flat on his tummy with his neck stretched out. She had heard the commotion and come out to investigate. He was badly winded, but luckily he had landed in some soft grass. Mrs Chattery stood looking at him, with her hands on her hips. Then she gazed up at the tree. Ma and Pa were flapping about and the three remaining babies were screaming even louder. The hole was far above her.

'You *silly* bird! There's no way I can put you back up there!' she said. 'Oh dear! *Now* what are we going to do with you?'

The baby bird's eyes flickered and he tried to lift his head. Mrs Chattery peered at him more closely. 'My, you *are* ugly,' she said. 'Plain hideous.'

Gingerly she picked him up. His squashy grey skin was all punctured with little tufty pinpoints where the feathers were starting to poke through. His neck was bare and scrawny and she could see the heartbeats through the thin skin on his chest. He opened his beak and wobbled his stumpy tongue at her. Mrs Chattery looked up to the tree where Ma and Pa were perched, watching her.

'Oh well, I'll do my best, ga-la-lahs!' she called up to them. 'Come on silly,' she said to the baby. 'Just as well you chose *my* gum tree to fall out of, for those people in Blotsville wouldn't know what to do with you.' Then she added, 'Silly me! They haven't any gum trees to fall out of anyway!'

•••••

14

Chapter 2

Seeds & a bit of spit

Abigail Chattery put the baby bird in a carton with a hot-water bottle wrapped in a pale pink angora cardigan. She hoped it would feel warm and downy like his mother's feathers. Then she gave him a drink of water from an eye-dropper. Most of it dribbled out of his beak ... 'But I think a little bit went down,' she said. 'Now for some food, and you needn't think I'm going to chew it up in my mouth like your mother does – oh, no. I'll use the whizzer.'

Using seeds and water and a bit of her own spit, she whizzed and stirred up a mushy mess and poked some down the baby's gaping throat with a tiny salt spoon before he knew what was happening. *Gulp.* Then, after all his adventures, he fell asleep.

'Now, what am I going to call him?' said Mrs Chattery to herself.

She thought of all the G names to go with galah ... Greg, Garry, George, Gladstone (after Mr Chattery) ... and then she remembered at school reading tales of King Arthur and his Knights of the Round Table. One of them, a knight in shining armour, had been Sir Galahad. 'That's it!' she cried, 'I'll call him Galahad! Galahad Galah!'

She stroked the ugly little bird. 'I hope you'll grow up to be as gorgeous as your mum and dad, and the sooner the better!' she crooned, looking at his bald grey skin. 'Thank goodness for feathers!'

Abigail was very good at raising birds. Galahad wolfed down the mushy meals that she whizzed up from seeds and spit, and soon he was able to nibble at seeds by himself. Luckily, sunflowers grew in the Chatterswood garden and Abigail stored the dried off heads in the shed, ready to feed to the chooks. With his strong beak and his grey, knobby tongue Galahad soon learned to crack open the black and white stripy seeds from the big flat sunflower heads.

He grew and grew. His feathers began to fluff and cover his squashy grey skin. 'Thank goodness for feathers!' sang Mrs Chattery, over and over again as she stroked the new feathers. 'What a *handsome* boy you are going to be!' Indeed, with his hot pink chest and his pale pink crest and his sleek grey back and his dark glittery eyes, Galahad was turning into a gorgeous, grown-up galah. Mrs Chattery talked to him all the time and he sometimes rode about on her shoulder.

For Abigail the best thing about galahs and cockatoos was their talk. They could be taught to copy things people said, soppy things like 'Who's a pretty boy, then?'. Abigail lost no time in training Galahad to utter such silly remarks and he was a quick learner, so that after a year or so of living with Abigail, Galahad was almost as talkative as she was. But, of course, he didn't understand what they were talking about because it was not Ga-la-language, it was People-speak.

If Abigail said to him, 'Who's a pretty boy, then?', he

would very likely reply, 'Down with Blotsville!' or 'Fatface!'. But Abigail and Galahad lived together very happily and had long and completely crazy conversations.

One day Ma and Pa left with the other three children, who had grown up safely and learned to fly. (They were all good little galahs and listened to their mother.) Just in case Galahad felt like going with them, Mrs Chattery clipped the flight feathers on one of his wings. This didn't hurt him, but it made him all lopsided and unable to fly.

'He's used to me,' she told herself. 'He'd never survive in the wild. Besides, a bird in the hand is worth two in the bush!' This was another saying she had read somewhere. 'And anyway,' she added, 'his wing feathers will grow again if he needs them.'

Although Galahad sometimes flapped his lopsided wings and gazed into the sky, he didn't seem to mind *much* not being able to fly, because he was used to Abigail and her sunflower seeds. And at last, after thirteen years, Abigail Chattery had someone to talk to.

•••

During this time, the houses and streets of Blotsville continued to spread over the countryside, the yellow paddocks vanishing under a jigsaw pattern of grey, red and brown rooftops.

The Bitzer family had moved into one of the new houses, one with a brown roof. Aaron and Lottie Bitzer owned the pet shop in the Blotsville shopping centre and as they spent most of their time in the shop and had little time for housework, they enjoyed their new home, with its time-saving gadgets and double garage and almost no garden space to be kept tidy.

But their children, Pippi and Max, soon found that

playing in their new suburb nearly always led to trouble.
If Max slogged a cricket ball it was likely to smash
through the neighbour's kitchen window and crunch her
microwave, or if he kicked his football too hard it would
flatten someone else's enormously expensive pot plant.
Noisy arguments would follow. Pippi could find nowhere
private, not even under a bush, to talk with her friends,
and kids weren't allowed to ride their skateboards in the
streets because of all the cars. So Pippi and Max often
went to the pet shop after school, to help with the
animals, or to mooch about in the town square where
there was a bit of space.

But one Sunday when the builders' trucks were off the
road, they decided to ride their bikes in the other
direction to investigate three big trees they could see
sticking up above the rooftops. They arrived outside

Chatterswood just in time to find Abigail Chattery at the gate muttering about blots on the landscape with Galahad bobbing up and down on her shoulder screeching 'Down with Blotsville!'

Max and Pippi climbed off their bikes and stared. They nudged one another and began to giggle.

Abigail stopped muttering. 'What are you two laughing at?' she demanded.

'You're funny, you and the galah!' said Pippi. 'Why are you going on about blots?'

'Why shouldn't I?' sniffed Abigail. 'Those houses … boxes, more like … they're spilling all over the paddocks, ruining the views with TV aerials and wires – I get mad as a snake.'

'We live in one of those boxes,' frowned Max. 'We can't help it.'

Mrs Chattery calmed down a bit. 'Oh dear, no I don't suppose you can.'

'Actually, they are a bit like boxes,' conceded Pippi. 'There's nowhere much to play.'

'There, I knew it,' said Mrs Chattery. 'Wait a bit and I'll get some ginger cake. You can talk to Galahad if you like, and see my garden, and then you can tell me who you are.'

Pippi and Max were used to birds in the pet shop, and they soon made friends with Galahad. Mrs Chattery's ginger cake was the best and they poked into the mysterious corners round the old house, and explored its rambling garden and its gum trees. 'There'd always be something to do here,' sighed Pippi. 'There's lots of secret places.'

'Then you must come again,' said Mrs Chattery, cutting some more cake, and Galahad yelled 'Joy and rapture! Who's a pretty boy?'

•••••

Chapter 3

Plank & Burpwistle's shady deal

Chatterswood was gradually hemmed in by the new houses. Along the smart new bitumen road running past its gate roared the builders' trucks and the concrete mixers and the earth movers, as well as a shiny red car belonging to the developer, Mr Bentley Plank. Whenever she saw the red car, Mrs Chattery quaked, for Bentley Plank knocked loudly on her door at least once a week offering to buy her land, and each time Mrs Chattery said she would never sell while she had breath in her body. And Galahad, sitting on her shoulder, would fix a beady eye on Mr Plank and call him Fatface or Ratbrain.

Bentley wondered if Mrs Chattery was a witch, with her screechy bird, but he had set his heart on her piece of land, so he ignored Galahad's rude remarks.

'I'll give you a good price, Mrs C., all fair and square, and you're sitting on a lovely block here, you know,' he wheedled. He didn't tell her how many houses he would be able to squash on the lovely block and the paddock she owned, once the old house and the gum trees were knocked down. He drooled when he thought of all the money he would make. 'Buy one and sell six – that's the way to do it,' he chortled to himself.

But how could he get the old witch-woman to move out? He encouraged his truckies to roar past her house at top speed or to slam on their air brakes near her gate or to drive on the gravel verges to stir up clouds of dust; but this only caused the newcomers in the surrounding houses to complain … and still Mrs Chattery wouldn't budge. So Bentley Plank said to himself, 'I'll go and see H. P.'

H. P. Burpwistle was the Mayor of Blotsville. He was also Bentley Plank's third cousin. He watched with pride as his town steadily rolled out across the country, smothering the paddocks with houses crammed together along new streets and courts and boulevards. It riled him that this smart new housing estate was spoiled by Mrs Chattery's shabby old cottage and its messy garden, with the three scruffy gum trees sticking up and ruining the neat, tidy skyline. 'It's a blot on the landscape!' he often said, and he said it again when Bentley Plank came to see him.

'Well, what can you do about it?' growled Bentley. 'That old witch-woman is holding up the tide of progress in this town.' He was rather proud of this remark and H. P. Burpwistle was impressed, too.

'You're dead right, Bent. Hm, I wonder …' mused H. P. 'What state is her old dump in … you know, the plumbing and the roof? Could it be called a health hazard?'

'Yair, easily!' grinned Bentley. 'The chimney's about to fall over – real dangerous – and the floors are sagging because the stumps are rotten, and the dunny's up the yard. It's a blot on the landscape, like you said. Shouldn't be allowed in this day and age.' Then Bentley remembered the pink parrot. 'And another thing,' he added. 'She lives with this bird, a nasty parrot thing … in the house, mind. It's not natural, is it? Think of the diseases!'

H. P. thought about diseases a lot; the very mention of germs and viruses freaked him out. 'I've heard enough!' he cried. 'Leave it to me, Bent … I'll have a word in the right ear,' said the Mayor of Blotsville.

Bentley Plank shook the Mayor's hand and slipped an envelope into his top pocket. 'Treat yourself to something a bit special, H. P.!' he winked. The envelope bulged with hundred-dollar notes.

H. P. Burpwistle patted his pocket. 'Well, ta very much, Bent … but just remember, we haven't had this conversation, have we.'

'What conversation do you mean, H. P.?' smirked Bentley Plank.

●●●

A week later, Mrs Chattery was visited by a building inspector from the Town Hall. He went all over the house and garden and scribbled notes on his clipboard.

'What's all this about? What are you doing?' asked Mrs Chattery.

'Just a routine check of your property, madam. I'm just doing my job,' answered the inspector, who didn't like to be asked questions.

In the mail a few days later Mrs Chattery received a council document stating that unless she had certain repairs and upgradings carried out, her house would be condemned as a dangerous structure and a health hazard.

The list of improvements and repairs included re-stumping the house, new floors, a new brick chimney, an indoor toilet connected to the town sewer, new roof guttering, complete re-wiring, demolition of the old cow shed (because of rats) and removal of three very old and dangerous gum trees. She was also warned about the risks of disease from parrots and other such birds and advised to confine her pet to a cage outdoors, or better still dispose of it altogether.

In a small paragraph at the end, it said, 'Unless these improvements are carried out in the next six months, the house will be due for demolition in accordance with the health and safety regulations.'

Abigail sank into a chair and felt faint. 'Demolition! Oh, Galahad!' she wailed, 'Whatever are we going to

do? How can I possibly pay for all those things? Six months! This is terrible!'

'Joy and rapture!' Galahad jigged on his perch.

'*No*! Galahad – it is not!' sobbed Mrs Chattery. 'It is misery and woe!'

Bentley Plank had kept watch that day for the postman to deliver Mrs Chattery's mail. Half an hour later he battered loudly on her door. She opened it with tears running down her cheeks and her breath coming in gasps, and Mr Plank knew he had her trapped.

'Good day to yer, Mrs C.,' he smirked. 'Have yer changed your mind yet?'

'I need time to think,' she whispered. 'Come back in a week, you … you nasty piece of work!'

Mr Plank looked shocked. '*Me*?' he gasped. 'How can

you say such a thing? Plank stands for progress in this town!'

'Piggy piggy Plank!' screeched Galahad, as Mrs Chattery banged the door.

From that day on, Abigail Chattery's heart felt wobbly. It lurched and bumped in her chest when she bent over, and she had to sit down and take deep breaths. She had pains in her arm.

'Dear me, Galahad,' she gasped. 'Something's not right. I'm not as young as I was, you know. And that Plank person has driven me to this!'

Galahad cocked his crest and bounced up and down and croaked, 'You won't get to first base,' which was not at all what Abigail wanted to hear just then, while her heart was wobbly.

'You might be right, you wretch,' she retorted. 'I'll have to go to the doctor.'

A bus now ran past the door along the smart new road, so Abigail took herself into Blotsville to see the doctor. The doctor listened to her heart through his stethoscope and said 'Ah' and 'Hum'.

'Have you been under any stress lately?' he asked.

'You bet I have,' sniffed Abigail. 'I'm surrounded by blots and plagued by Plank's Progress.'

'This old girl must be dotty,' the doctor thought to himself. 'She's seeing things! Blots?' Out loud he told her that she could no longer live by herself, for her heart was not strong enough for jobs like scrubbing floors and weeding the sunflowers. 'You will have to go into a retirement home, where you can be looked after,' he said. And he rang up the Manager of the new Dreamydays Rest Home, who luckily had a space.

Mrs Chattery could think of no other solution to all her problems. She was forced to sell Chatterswood to Bentley Plank, give away her furniture, pack up her belongings and move into the Dreamydays Rest Home in Blotsville. Bentley Plank rang up H. P. Burpwistle and hissed, 'She's going! Demolition starts next week, if you're interested!'

Mayor Burpwistle went personally to watch as Mr Plank's bulldozers thundered along the road and crunched Chatterswood up into splintery little bits which were then burnt on a bonfire in the middle of the garden. H. P. advised Bentley Plank to leave the gum trees where they were for the moment, as some of the neighbours were rather wild about the clouds of smelly smoke and he didn't want to upset them further. The three old gum trees could wait a bit, but their turn would soon come. He beamed with satisfaction when he thought of the six new houses, all crammed together, which would soon replace shabby old Chatterswood. And he patted his top pocket, into which Bentley Plank had slipped another fat envelope.

When Max and Pippi next rode down to Chatterswood, all they found was a big black heap of ashes.

•••••

Chapter 4

No birds for Dreamydays

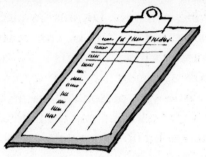

The Dreamydays Rest Home was on a hill overlooking
the Blotsville housing estate. From there, not far away,
Mrs Chattery's three gum trees were still visible in a
space among the jigsaw roofs.

Dreamydays was known as a 'State-of-the-art Aged
Care Facility', which meant that it was brand new and
very smart and extremely tidy, and not a bit like
Chatterswood. It had a brand new and very smart and
extremely tidy Manager, as well.

When Mrs Chattery arrived at Dreamydays in a taxi,
Galahad was in his carry-cage on top of her luggage. The
Manager came to the entrance to meet the new arrival.
She carried a red clipboard and was so busy jotting on it
that she didn't notice the birdcage. 'Welcome to
Dreamydays, Mrs Chattery,' she said to the old lady. 'I
know you are going to be happy here, making lots of
new friends, aren't you!'

'How would I know?' said Mrs Chattery, who was
still feeling shocked and wobbly. 'I mightn't get to first
base. Can I have a pink bedspread, please?'

The Manager consulted her clipboard. 'No, you are

going into the Blue Wing, where you'll have a blue bedspread and blue curtains and be very happy,' she answered, firmly.

Galahad, looking as pink as possible, inspected her with his glinty eyes and said 'Twerp!', before letting out an ear-splitting galah-shriek.

The Manager jumped and her face changed from smiley to steely. 'What is that ... *bird* doing here?' she demanded, pointing at him with her ballpoint pen.

'He's Galahad, my friend,' explained Abigail. 'He goes everywhere with me.'

'Ah *no*, he doesn't ... not any longer,' replied the Manager. 'You didn't mention him before! Birds are *not allowed* at Dreamydays!' She wrote furiously on her red clipboard.

'Blot blot blot fatty fatface!!' shrieked Galahad, dancing on his perch.

The Manager drew herself up very tall. 'What a *rude* bird! He must go ... at once! This instant! We don't have that sort of coarse language at Dreamydays!'

Mrs Chattery clutched at her chest. 'But ... I've heard that some people in rest homes have their cats, or dogs, so I thought it would be all right if Galahad came! I've had him for ages ... I raised him myself after he fell out of his nest. I saved his life ... didn't I, Galahad ... he's house trained and I need him to talk to!'

An old man shuffled past on a walking stick and saw Galahad. 'Who's a pretty boy, then?' he crooned and, poking his bent fingers through the cage bars, he tickled the galah's head. Galahad closed his eyes and went all floppy. 'I used to have a white cocky m'self, called Sulf,' said the old man to Abigail. 'You know, "Sulf" because

he was a sulphur-crested cocky. Had him for years and years … what a card he was! Just like one of the family!'

'Yes, Mr Blunt, no doubt he was,' interrupted the Manager, 'but now, I think it's time for your rest.'

'It is not!' Mr Blunt was not going to be ordered about. 'And how come this galah's moving in here, eh?' he growled at the Manager. 'I had to send Sulf to the pet shop because you told *me* pets weren't allowed!'

'And neither they are,' snapped the Manager, 'par-tic-u-lar-ly parrots, and this bird will be off to the pet shop too, just as soon as I've made a phone call to Mr Bitzer.'

•••

The new Blotsville shopping centre was built around a square with a council garden in the middle. One old, spreading gum tree right in the centre had been kept to remind the citizens of Blotsville that they lived in Australia, but when one of its boughs fell off, Mayor Burpwistle had the tree cut down in case someone was hit on the head and sued the council. So all that was left of the garden were some very straight beds with tidy rows of orange and purple flowers and a line of pointy young cypress trees.

The pet shop owned by Aaron and Lottie Bitzer was

at one corner of the square, next to the Blotsville Bank. At first Aaron and Lottie had named their shop 'Fur, Feathers, Fins & Fangs', but this was far too tongue-twisty for the shoppers, so the name was painted out and replaced with a big twirly gold sign saying, 'Bitzers', which is what everyone called it anyway. There was always a queue of people lined up at the Blotsville Bank, next door, to use the auto-teller, so Aaron Bitzer kindly entertained them while they queued by filling his pet shop window with fluffy kittens, bright budgies and golden fish, and very often, when the people had drawn their money out of the auto-teller, they went into Bitzers and spent some of it. So almost everyone in Blotsville had a pet or two, except for the old people at the Dreamydays Rest Home.

In a yard at the back of the shop, Aaron kept spare cages and boxes where he cared for stray, sick or injured animals and birds, for he was very soft-hearted. Too soft-hearted, Lottie sometimes thought as she helped to care for magpies with broken wings or orphan baby possums.

On the afternoon of Mrs Chattery's arrival at Dreamydays, Aaron Bitzer was summoned to the Rest Home by the Manager. 'We have a new resident, and her parrot needs to be disposed of, at once,' she announced on the phone. 'Can you come?'

'Okay,' said Aaron, who had done this sort of thing for the Manager before.

'Who is the owner of the parrot?'

'A Mrs Chattery. These cases are very difficult,' she added.

Aaron hung up and sighed. 'They sure are,' he said, wondering what he would tell Max and Pippi, who had already been in tears about Mrs Chattery and Galahad having to leave Chatterswood. The children had just come in from school and he decided to take them with him to Dreamydays.

The Manager was waiting for them and Galahad was in his cage by the front entrance, scattering seed all over the porch.

'Would you please remove this obnoxious bird!' the Manager demanded, pointing at Galahad. 'Look at the filthy mess!'

The children rushed to the cage and began scratching his head and talking to him.

'Now, he's a pretty decent galah, he is,' said Aaron, also having a scratch. 'Very nice.'

'Goody gum trees,' croaked Galahad, who enjoyed tickles.

'He's a terrific talker,' said Max. 'Why can't he stay here? Poor Mrs Chattery … she's already lost her home.'

'We don't allow pets,' replied the Manager, 'par-tic-u-lar-ly parrots. They are a serious health risk, they are noisy and this par-tic-u-lar parrot is extremely rude!'

'I get the picture,' growled Aaron, 'although he wouldn't thank you for calling him a parrot when he's a galah. You can tell Mrs Chattery that I'll see he's well looked after. Does she want to say goodbye to him?'

'Oh, no, I shouldn't think so,' said the Manager. 'She's shut herself in her room and doesn't want to be disturbed. I expect she's unpacking.'

'Huh!' grunted Aaron, who guessed that Mrs Chattery was more likely to be crying her eyes out. He looked around. 'Now, where have those kids got to?'

Pippi had found a list of residents' names and room numbers on a notice board in the foyer. Mrs Chattery's

room was Blue 7. 'Come on!' she hissed to Max, and they vanished along a corridor with a blue carpet and knocked on the door of number 7. Inside they found Mrs Chattery sitting on her bed in a very blue room and mopping her eyes with a pink handkerchief. When she saw the children, she sobbed aloud.

'Oh, what are you two doing here?' she wailed.

'It's all right, Mrs Chattery ... we've come to collect Galahad. We know it's not fair, but we'll look after him for you,' said Max.

'You can come and visit him sometimes, Mum and Dad wouldn't mind,' said Pippi, who had just thought of this. 'At least he knows us, and we won't let Dad sell him. We've still got Sulf, and he came from Dreamydays, ages ago.'

Mrs Chattery blew her nose like a trumpet, then patted Pippi's arm. 'Oh, I know – Sulf belonged to old Mr Blunt. But thank you both,' she sniffed. 'You've made me feel a little bit better. Will you come and see me sometimes?'

'Course we will,' said Max, who was embarrassed by all these tears.

'Come on Pip, Dad'll be looking for us.'

They ran back to the entrance and found Aaron picking up Galahad's cage ready for departure. 'Hurry up kids, where have you been?' he said. 'Let's take Galahad to meet Sulf.'

As they left, Galahad puffed up very pink and glared at the Manager. 'Blot blot blotface!' he shouted. 'Thank goodness for feathers!'

•••••

Galahad & Sulf at Bitzers

Mrs Lottie Bitzer fell in love with Galahad as soon as Aaron carried him into the shop.

'Joy and rapture!' was Galahad's opening remark, a favourite saying of Mrs Chattery's.

'*Who's* a pretty boy, then?' crooned Lottie. 'Oh, Aaron, he's gorgeous!'

'Yeah … another refugee from the Rest Home,' snapped Aaron. 'Poor old Abigail Chattery. She didn't even get to say goodbye to him.'

'Oh dear, that's cruel,' said Lottie. '*Poor* Mrs Chattery. Dreamydays must seem like a prison to her, after her dear old home.' She stroked Galahad's grey back. 'Do we need to sell him? He could stay here, like Sulf, and keep him company. And then maybe Mrs Chattery and Mr Blunt could come and visit them sometimes!'

'We've already told Mrs Chattery that,' interrupted Pippi, 'and it cheered her up a bit.'

'Hold on … don't rush things,' said her father. 'Sulf might not like him.'

Aaron and Lottie took Galahad out of his cage and

inspected him all over from feet to beak, in case he had anything wrong, but they could find nothing. Although his wing was clipped, his eyes were bright and smiley, his feathers rich and sleek, his four-toed scaly feet were strong, and his crest and cheek feathers fluffed up pink when he squawked.

Galahad cocked his head in all directions and inspected his new surroundings. He'd never seen so many creatures all at once. There were mewling kittens, yapping puppies, chattering budgies, whistling canaries, chumbling hamsters, fish waving their tails and finches zipping between their perches. Galahad felt quite giddy and the noise was deafening, a pandemonium of barks and screeches and whistles. How he longed to be back at peaceful Chatterswood among the gum trees. He let out an anxious shriek and flapped his lopsided grey wings to show their pink undersides, but none of the other creatures took any notice of him.

'You're a *booodiful* boy,' sang Lottie, snuggling him up to her neck. 'A scrumptious galah!'

'Aw, come on Mum!' protested Max. 'He's not a cream cake! Put him in his cage for a while, until he gets used to us.' He hung it up by the counter and Lottie placed Galahad inside it.

Galahad sidled to and fro along his perch, peering anxiously through the bars, but when Lottie gave him a potful of sunflower seeds to nibble, he began to feel a little more at home.

•••

Sulf was the biggest attraction at Bitzers and he was not for sale. Shoppers and motorists, bank tellers and children, the butcher, the pharmacist, the dentist's nurse and the bus driver all went out of their way to visit Bitzers and to talk to Sulf. Sulf was king of the Blotsville shopping centre. He could be heard from all corners of the square if he raised his voice, for Sulf was the whitest, screechiest sulphur-crested cockatoo you have ever seen or heard.

On fine days, Sulf sat on his stand just outside the shop door so that he could see what was going on in the square and talk to people as they passed by or waited in the bank queue. He was secured to his stand by a light chain so that nobody could carry him off. At first, Aaron had used a length of cord, but Sulf liked nothing better than a piece of cord to chew through, so Aaron used the chain.

When Sulf had belonged to Mr Blunt, before he came to the Bitzers, he had learned a fine collection of army phrases like 'Quick march!' and 'Eyes right!' and 'Halt!' because Mr Blunt had once been a soldier. Later Sulf had copied other words he heard in the shop, like 'Canary seed! Canary seed!' and 'Four dollars fifty – ping!' Like Galahad, Sulf had his wing clipped so that he couldn't fly away and, like Galahad, Sulf was a very talkative bird.

But later that day, when Aaron carried Galahad's cage out and hung it up near Sulf's perch, the two birds stared at one another for a long time in silence. Neither of them said a word – they just sidled along their perches and cocked their heads at one another. Finally, Sulf let out an ear-splitting shriek which could be heard right across the square and Galahad did a big noisy wing-flap and began to mumble very softly in Ga-la-language.

Now, Sulf did not speak Ga-la-language – he spoke Cocka-talk, but they could understand each other quite well in their slightly different accents. Very soon they knew everything they needed to know about one another, and the main thing Galahad needed to know was that Sulf was boss.

'Okay, pink bird,' said Sulf in Cocka-talk, 'just remember that I'm bigger than you, and I got here first, and I'm white, and my crest is bigger than yours – it's truly gorgeous.' He snapped open his brilliant crest feathers like a golden fan.

Although Galahad thought that white was rather boring and that a sulphur yellow crest was not as charming as pale pink, he wisely decided to let Sulf be boss for the time being and very soon he was learning to say 'Canary seed!' and 'Quick march!' and 'Left turn!', while Sulf was practising phrases like 'Twerpface!' and 'Goody gum trees!'

One day Lottie heard Galahad shout, 'Hoo-ray, hoo-rah for the ga-la-lah!' and she made up a special shout for Sulf, too, so that he wouldn't feel left out. Soon the people in the bank queue were enjoying a new bird duet, which went –

Hoo-ray, hoo-rah for the ga-la-lah!
Hoo-roo for the cock-a-too!

The queues outside Bitzers grew longer and slower. People came by from all over the square and from further afield, even when they didn't need to go to the bank.

•••

In the past, when Pippi and Max had visited the pet shop after school, they had enjoyed parading around the Blotsville town square with Sulf riding on their shoulders. They called this Sulf's Outing. Pippi would take him as far as the gum tree stump in the middle of

the gardens, and Max would carry him back to the shop. They would let him sit on the stump where he could nibble at the dead bark and sharpen his beak, flap his wings and screech like a factory whistle to frighten away the sparrows. People around the square would nod and say, 'There's Sulf having his outing!'

Aaron was happy about Sulf's outings, because they were a walking advertisement for his shop, and he thought it would now be an even better advertisement if Galahad went too. It also meant that Pippi and Max had a bird each to carry and they no longer had to fight about taking turns.

'Now look after this galah and watch out for stray dogs,' Aaron warned. Each bird had a chain attached to one leg, with the other end round the child's wrist for safety. Sometimes, when Sulf and Galahad flapped and screeched and stretched their wings and bodies, it seemed to Pippi and Max that they were trying to fly up into the sky.

'I think it's a bit mean,' Pippi told Max. 'You know, keeping them on chains like this. What would happen if we let them go? Birds are meant to fly.'

'They mightn't come back,' said Max, 'and then we'd be for it! Dad always says they'd probably die in the wild, 'cause they're not used to it. Anyway, their wing feathers are clipped, they couldn't fly even if they wanted to. And they've never had any practice.'

'Poor things,' sighed Pippi, stroking Galahad's back. 'It must feel like us being in a wheelchair – you know, not able to walk. I wish *I* could fly, wow – I dream about it sometimes. You know, zooming around up there in the wind and looking down on houses and towns and tiny people like ants, and going wherever you want to, instead of having boring outings like this.'

'Yeah, awesome,' grunted Max.

Galahad and Sulf flapped and screeched some more and all the people round the town square smiled and said, 'That'll be Sulf and Galahad having their outing. Aren't they lucky birds!'

•••••

Chapter 6

Burpwistle's megablunder

As well as encouraging his third cousin Bentley Plank to build housing estates and to chop down dangerous trees, H. P. Burpwistle, the Mayor, had other progressive plans for Blotsville, too. First, he wanted to close down the fresh food market and use the space for a car park, which was badly needed. The market was the oldest part of Blotsville, having been started by farmers who brought their fresh fruit, vegetables and poultry in from the country before there were many shops in the new suburbs. The stalls were piled high with brightly coloured lemons, pumpkins, tomatoes, beetroot, watermelons and spinach, and the flower stalls were fragrant with boronia and daffodils, and the smell from the homemade bread stall drew customers from blocks away.

H. P. Burpwistle, however, had been nervous about fresh food markets ever since his childhood, when he had suffered a frightful tummy upset. He had vomited and vomited until he thought he would turn inside out. The doctor had said, 'This lad has food poisoning.

What has he been eating?' And his mother had replied, 'It must have been something I bought at the fresh food market.'

Mrs Burpwistle was quite wrong, for H. P.'s tummy upset was caused by a dirty, germy knife which she had used to slice meat for his school sandwich, but she didn't know that and neither did anyone else. From that day onwards, Mrs Burpwistle had always blamed the fresh food market for H. P.'s food poisoning and H. P. had always believed that the market was crawling with huge, hairy germs that attacked tummies. He had become very thin and anxious. Now that he was Mayor, he had his chance to get rid of the market and all its germs and to cover the whole place in concrete. Bentley Plank would be able to help him – he was an expert concreter.

The Mayor's other plan was to remove Bitzers' Pet Shop from the town square. He felt sure that even nastier, hairier germs were spreading from the birdcages and litter trays all round the town centre and that an epidemic of something vomitous was bound to befall the town soon. He was furious to learn that Mrs Chattery's pink parrot had moved to the town centre and was now in league with Sulf. As well as hating fresh food markets, H. P. Burpwistle also hated cockatoos, for he had once put his finger into a cocky's cage and had it severely chewed – almost off – he still carried the scar. To H. P. Burpwistle, cockatoos, like germs, were a serious danger to the public.

Mayor Burpwistle ordered his Town Planner to design a new corner for the square. The Town Planner's name was Gilbert Culvert and he didn't always like H. P. Burpwistle's plans, but he didn't dare to disagree with

them in case he lost his job. He had four little Culverts at
home to feed.

The market was just behind Bitzers, which was lucky.
'Now, see here,' said the Mayor to the Town Planner,
pointing to the map, 'if Bitzers' shop were to be
bulldozed flat, we could disinfect the site, get rid of the
germs, and then concrete over the lot and make it the
entrance to the new car park, that is after we disinfect the
old market site. It's just beyond the square and beside the
Blotsville Bank, so there's everything anybody could
need – car park, money, shops. What more could they
want? It's perfect!'

The Mayor was so sure that his plan was perfect that
he told Gilbert Culvert, the Town Planner, to keep it
secret – it would come as a wonderful surprise for the
town council and for the people of Blotsville … and
H. P. Burpwistle would be famous.

The plans were drawn up, and Mayor Burpwistle
decided to display them in the square and to launch his
Big Surprise with a jazz band and speeches one Saturday
morning when the town was full of shoppers. A small
stage would be put up and covered with a gaily striped
awning. The band would assemble on the lawn nearby,
playing bouncy tunes to put the people in a happy mood.
There would be a sausage sizzle, of course, and balloons.
The Bitzer family decided to invite Mrs Chattery and Mr
Blunt to visit the shop that day and to have a sausage-
sizzle lunch party with Galahad and Sulf.

When the day came, Pippi and Max took the two birds
for an early outing and then joined the crowd to hear the
Mayor's announcement on the way back. The platform
was near the Bitzers' corner of the square in front of the

pointy young cypress trees. Its red and white striped awning gleamed in the sun; there were plastic ferns and a microphone stood at the front of the stage. On the lawn, the band were settling themselves, shuffling their music and yawning, for they weren't used to performing so early in the day. The barbecues were firing up and bunches of balloons bounced about on light poles. The new plans were displayed on a large pin board near the stage. Nobody was bothering to look at them yet, for the people who were strolling into the park were more interested in the sausages and balloons and the warm sunshine. Lottie Bitzer left Aaron to mind the shop while she led Mrs Chattery and Mr Blunt to some chairs in the front row by the stage. Further along the row sat Bentley Plank, for the Mayor had let him know that the Big Surprise would be of interest to him, as it involved concrete and demolition.

•••

At eleven o'clock the band played a screechy fanfare and the Mayor, H. P. Burpwistle, wearing his robes and gold chain, climbed onto the platform, accompanied by the Town Planner and three councillors. The Town Planner, Gilbert Culvert, looked nervous, and the councillors didn't really know why they were there. Crowds were gathering round, so Pippi and Max stayed in the shelter of the cypress trees behind the platform in case Galahad and Sulf took fright. The two birds perched on low branches and began to poke about.

'Good morning, citizens of Blotsville!' the Mayor sang into the microphone. 'And what a good morning it is! For years I have had a vision for our town centre and on this beautiful morning I am going to let you into my secret!

My vision is first and foremost to protect your health. Today you have your chance to see my wonderful plans and to express your support for them.' He stuck out his skinny chest and stroked his gold chain.

A voice from the tree croaked, quite softly, 'Who's a pretty boy then?'

'Shut up, Sulf!' hissed Pippi.

Sulf didn't want to shut up. '*Who's* a pretty boy then?' he said, much louder. 'Pretty boy pretty boy pretty boy!!'

The crowd began to titter, and then to laugh as Galahad joined in. '*Who's* a pretty boy, eh? Fatface! Fatface!'

The two birds rocked up and down in their tree, tossing the words to each other, getting more and more screechy as the crowd smiled and murmured. H. P. Burpwistle was not only furious at being interrupted, but

suddenly he also felt rather silly, dressed up in his robes
and chain like a 'pretty boy' in fancy dress, while
everyone else wore T-shirts and jeans and laughed at him.

'It's those blasted parrots,' he muttered to himself.
'Where the devil are they? I'll strangle them!'

Nobody could see where they were – they were hidden
in the dense cypress tree where, trailing their long chains,
they were gradually climbing higher to get a better view.

The noise calmed down and the Mayor tried again.
He had reached his pet topic of hairy germs and stomach
infections, and he began to warn the crowd about the
dangers of fresh food markets.

'What about sausage sizzles?' shouted a man, for the
tummy-tickling smell from the barbecues was causing
mouths to water.

'Cats meat!' shrieked Sulf.

'Ha!' the crowd chuckled.

'Four dollars fifty – ping, ping, *ping*!' screeched Galahad.

Raising his voice, the Mayor tried to move on to his next point, that keeping animals and birds in a shopping centre was even more unhygienic than selling fruit and vegetables in the open air.

The crowd's good-natured laughter began to turn to frowns and low muttering. The three councillors on stage, who had known nothing of the Mayor's plans, were whispering among themselves. Lottie Bitzer ran to fetch Aaron. 'Quick, lock up the shop, Aaron, and come and listen to this! Burpwistle's ratting on us, I reckon!'

As Aaron followed her out, he heard a woman yell, 'You can't do that … the pet shop's been here since the square was built and we've never caught the plague before – and what about Sulf and Galahad? They're Blotsville's mascots!'

'*Hear hear*!' came the shout. Someone picked up an old gumnut and hurled it towards the stage, where it clonked Gilbert Culvert on the head.

Aaron had turned white. 'What's going on?' he gasped.

'He's trying to close us down, that's what,' hissed Lottie, 'and the market, too. I told you, he's a rat!'

By now the people were elbowing in towards the display board to look at the plans. 'Look here! It's a car park where the market should be – and see! Bitzers has gone too – there's a roadway instead, into the car park!'

Someone called out, rather feebly, 'Well, we *need* a bigger car park! And we don't need the old market when we've got the Monstermart! It's got music and airconditioning and stuff.'

He was shouted down. 'So *what*! I got some *beaudiful* fresh rhubarb at the market …'

'And what about the flowers!'

'Where else can you get fresh artichokes? Or pea straw? Or proper eggs? Or chook manure?'

H. P. Burpwistle turned pale green at the mention of manure.

Galahad began to scream, 'Blothead! Canary seed! Goody gum trees!' and Max grabbed him tight in case he fell off the branch.

But Sulf was now silent. He had spied something higher up the tree and was inching his way towards it – a piece of rope knotted round the trunk. Pippi felt his chain dragging at her wrist. 'What's up, Sulf? What are you doing?' she whispered.

Sulf had reached the knot and started to attack the rope, tearing at the fibres with all his might. Galahad was now screeching, 'Pretty boy! Ha ha ha!'

'What's Sulf found?' asked Max.

'Some old rope to chew,' said Pippi.

Max peered up through the branches. 'That's not an old rope!' he hissed. 'It's tying up the awning!'

Pippi peered through to the platform and gasped. The other end of the rope was attached to one corner of the striped canvas above the Mayor's head. 'Ow!' she squeaked, 'Stop it Sulf, it'll all collapse!'

'No, don't stop him,' whispered Max. 'Look!' He pointed to another tree along the row. 'There's the rope from the other corner. Come on Galahad, you can have a go at that one!' Max carried him to the second tree, and bits of fibre and fluff were soon flying in all directions. The awning began to sway and wobble.

The Mayor sighed with relief when those raucous shouts from the tree suddenly stopped, and he turned again to the noisy crowd in front. Holding up his hand for silence, he tried again to explain the dangers of hairy germs, but the yells and boos grew louder, and the two policemen on duty gripped their batons nervously in case a riot broke out.

Suddenly there was a swishing in the tree and a piece of rope came snaking out from among the branches and hit the ground with a *thwack!* The awning wobbled and teetered for a moment, until a second piece of rope flew out, *thwunk!* and the whole canvas fell to the stage, knocking over the microphone and several plastic ferns and enveloping the Mayor, the Town Planner and the three councillors in red and white striped canvas. As they thrashed about and tangled their legs in ropes and chairs and the microphone cord, the crowd's rage turned to stunned silence and then a huge wave of laughter. This was even better than a circus!

The band struck up some hot jazz and many people began dancing on the grass, while others knocked over the display boards and then rushed to the sausage sizzle.

The Mayor and his team struggled out from beneath the heaving canvas. H. P. Burpwistle's slicked-back hair was now all over his crimson face and his chain had broken and was dangling down near his bony knees. Before he could pull himself together, the three councillors confronted him.

'How dare you embarrass us like that!' yelled one.

'Why didn't you present your plans to council first?'

demanded the second. 'We could have told you they'd never work – look at the crowd! They think you're a joke! A clown!'

'You've just lost yourself the next election!' roared the third. 'You and your gastric germs! How did you ever get to be Mayor? You're a disaster! You'll be forced to resign!'

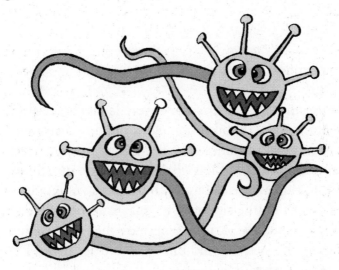

Bentley Plank, with a face like thunder, slipped through the crowd and vanished back to his red car. Without Burpwistle as Mayor, he would find it much more difficult to get permits for his shonky plans. 'The fool!' he fumed. 'If he gets kicked out, I'll be ruined!'

Aaron and Lottie stormed up to the platform to add their protests, followed by Mrs Chattery and Mr Blunt, waving his walking-stick. He spied the microphone lying among the wreckage, seized it and bellowed, 'Testing, testing! One, two, one two … can you hear me?'

'Yes!' roared the crowd.

'Atten-shun!' boomed Mr Blunt, in his loudest army parade-ground voice. 'This has been a load of codswallop! What has it been?'

'*A load of codswallop!*' echoed the crowd.

'Whadderwewant?' Mr Blunt went on.

'*Bitzers to stay*!!'

'Whendowewantit?'

'*Now!*'

'Whadderwewant?'

'*The Market to stay*!!'

'Whendowewantit?'

'*Now!*'

Press and TV camera crews were feverishly flashing and filming and mobile-phoning through to their offices to say, 'Hold the headlines – we've got a hot story! Threat of killer germs! Riot in Blotsville! Burpwistle's megablunder!'

H. P. Burpwistle tottered off the stage wiping his sweaty face on the sleeve of his mayoral robe. 'Those blithering, beastly parrots, where *are* they?' he roared, scanning the trees behind him. 'I'll murder them! I'll roast them alive!' He was shaking with rage.

But when the awning collapsed, Pippi and Max had grabbed the two birds and fled through the crowd and back to the pet shop. Before H. P. Burpwistle had untangled himself, Galahad and Sulf were back on their perches, surrounded by sausage-eating fans. The market stalls and Aaron's shop had never done such a roaring trade as they did that Saturday, and Mrs Chattery and Mr Blunt told everyone they had never had such a wonderful day out.

'Better than a circus,' said Abigail Chattery.

•••••

Chapter 7

Gloria Gusto's think tank

Blotsville was in turmoil for days after the H. P. Burpwistle disaster. At a special emergency meeting, the town council passed a vote of no confidence in the Mayor and he was forced to resign. He had nightmares about giant purple hairy germs and man-eating cockatoos and he had to go away to the seaside for a rest cure.

The council voted for a new Mayor and elected Councillor Gloria Gusto. Mrs Gusto's family owned two dogs, three Burmese cats, fourteen goldfish and a family of hamsters (all bought from Bitzers after various visits to the bank) and every Tuesday she did her shopping at the fresh food market (which her father-in-law Giovanni supplied with onions and tomatoes from his market garden). She filled her house with flowers and fruit, and was not worried in the least about big, hairy germs.

One morning during breakfast at Dreamydays, old Mr Blunt put down his copy of *The Blotsville Bugle* and said to Mrs Chattery, 'Things seem to be settling down … but you know, Abigail, we oughta strike while the iron's hot.'

'Whatever do you mean, Bertie?' asked Mrs Chattery, spreading jam.

'Look, we might have saved the pet shop and the market for the moment, but there's still plenty wrong with this town.'

'D'you mean things like blots and Plank's Progress?' asked Mrs Chattery. 'And my dear old cottage being bashed and burnt? And other people living in boxes?' She fished out her pink handkerchief and dabbed her eyes.

'I do,' said Mr Blunt, 'and people like us living here with nothing to do when we could be doing something. We could start a Better Blotsville Brigade. Someone has to stand up to reptiles like that Plank fella.'

'How?' asked Mrs Chattery. 'Who'd take any notice of oldies like us?'

'Not just us, we need some others, like the Bitzers for a start. They'll be worried about their shop. And I reckon Gloria Gusto might just listen, especially after what happened to Burpwistle.'

Mr Blunt decided to make some phone calls straight after breakfast. 'I'm going into action!' he said, pushing back his chair.

First he rang Bitzers and talked to Aaron, and Aaron said he would talk to Lottie and the kids. Then he rang the Town Hall and, after a bit of arguing, was put through to Mayor Gusto. After listening to Mr Blunt's account of what was wrong with Blotsville and especially with Bentley Plank's idea of progress, Mrs Gusto said, 'I think we need to have a small conference. Would you and Mrs Chattery be able to come and speak for the older citizens, do you think?'

'We'll be there,' said Mr Blunt eagerly, 'and I tell you what, Mayor, we'll round up the Bitzer family to represent the rest, kids and all.'

'Excellent!' Mayor Gusto believed in asking people what they wanted, unlike ex-Mayor Burpwistle who had always told people what he thought was good for them (and especially good for himself and Bentley Plank).

The conference was quickly arranged for a couple of days later, after school, and Mayor Gusto ordered chocolate mud cake and vanilla slices for afternoon tea in her big, shiny office. A large silver car was sent to fetch Mrs Chattery and Mr Blunt from Dreamydays. Mrs Chattery had dressed herself all in pink, with a feathery hat, and Mr Blunt wore his army medals.

'We're going to a conference with the Mayor at the Town Hall,' explained Mrs Chattery to the startled Manager, as the chauffeur opened the car door for them.

'Whatever for?' gasped the Manager.

'To launch the Better Blotsville Brigade, that's what for,' growled Mr Blunt. 'This town needs help.'

The Manager frowned, but she felt sure the conference had nothing to do with her State-of-the-art Aged Care Facility.

Lottie Bitzer made both the children scrub their knees and faces and comb their hair after school, while Aaron closed up the shop and stuck a notice on the door saying '*Back soon – gone to the Town Hall*'.

The children thought that Galahad and Sulf should have been invited to the meeting, especially after their spectacular success in wrecking the Burpwistle Plan, but Lottie shook her head.

'Don't be silly my darlings,' she said. 'Galahad and

Sulf wouldn't know a community plan if they perched on one. And they might make a mess in the Mayor's office. But I'm sure they will come in handy later.'

Mayor Gusto came out to the foyer of the Town Hall to greet them all. She was dressed in yellow and her cheerful voice rang round the lofty walls as she led them through to her office. After they'd eaten the mud cake and vanilla slices, the children were encouraged to go into the mayoral powder room to wash. They tried all the different soaps – six sorts.

'Now,' said the Mayor, when at last everyone was settled. 'I am new in this job and I want to know if things are not right in our town, so you are here to tell me. She turned to Max and Pippi. 'Kids first,' she decided, before they started to fidget.

Pippi felt shy, but Max sailed right in. 'There's no room to play round our place,' he said. 'I'm always busting things next door and the neighbours get really mad.'

'And there's nowhere to go with friends to be by ourselves, except the footpaths and the square. No quiet places,' added Pippi, nervously.

'You've got your own bedroom,' said her mother in surprise.

'Then you're always calling out for me to set the table or something,' muttered Pippi. 'I mean somewhere else.'

'I know, dear,' said Mrs Chattery. 'Like up a tree or under a big bush or in an old shed.' Pippi nodded at her and thought of Chatterswood.

Max interrupted, 'Well, I'd like a bike track or a skateboard park.'

'They're no good for older people,' objected Aaron.

'That's right,' said Mr Blunt, rubbing his knee so hard that his medals jingled. 'Bike tracks are no use to us with our creaky joints, but I know what Max means – kids want somewhere to go and space to do things like kicking balls, and I want something to do, too. Not to be plonked in front of a telly all day or let out to just hobble up and down a path looking at straight lines of orange marigolds.'

'Well, I'd like a pet,' said Mrs Chattery. 'Mr Blunt and I do miss our cockies, and I miss my view, too, and my old goody gum trees.'

Mayor Gusto sighed. 'Cockatoo pets might be a problem in a Rest Home, I'm afraid. Um ... a bit too noisy, don't you think?'

'I s'pose so,' growled Mr Blunt. 'Anyway, our Manager wouldn't have it. She's a parrot hater.'

'What about you, Lottie? Aaron?' asked the Mayor.

'Well, you know what our worry is – that the shop will be closed, now that Burpwistle has stirred up the idea,' sighed Aaron.

'But I miss another thing in our new suburb,' said Lottie. 'If I run out of milk at home or want to post a letter, I have to get in the car and drive all the way to the Monstermart or the square. There's nowhere I can walk to like a corner shop with a mailbox outside. No wonder we all need cars and grow fat and don't get to meet anyone in the street. Who plans these estates?'

'Rascals like Bentley Plank plan them,' growled Mr Blunt, 'and their first priority is to make a big fat profit. Think what he did to poor Abigail and her place through some hanky-panky deal with the council I reckon ... and as soon as he's axed the trees he going to cram six houses in, *six*!' By the time he'd finished, Mrs Chattery was in tears again. Lottie sat beside her and patted her hand.

Mrs Gusto's brown eyes had widened as Mr Blunt told the tale, and now she stood up, saying, 'Excuse me a moment – I'll be back.' She strode straight to the planning department and ordered that no permit was to be issued to build on Mrs Chattery's land or to cut down any trees until the situation had been investigated. She didn't know what Mr Blunt meant by a hanky-panky deal, but it all smelled very fishy to Mrs Gusto.

When she heard this, Mrs Chattery blew her nose and cried, 'Oh, thank you Madam Mayor! Do you really think you can save my trees?'

Mrs Gusto couldn't promise anything but said she'd have a jolly good try. 'Now,' she went on, shuffling through all her notes and scribbles. 'I have taken all your ideas on board and I will discuss them with the proper people at the Town Hall and, of course, with the council. I'll call another meeting with you all soon to tell you what is happening – and to hear any new ideas you might have, too.'

Aaron was staring. 'Is this really the way councils work?' he asked.

'This isn't the council,' beamed Mayor Gusto, 'this is a Think Tank!'

•••••

Chapter 8

Who's going to pay for it?

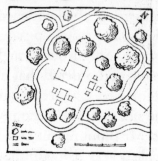

Mrs Gusto's first step was to pay a mayoral visit to the Dreamydays Rest Home to see what the two old people were complaining about. 'I would so like to inspect your state-of-the-art facilities for myself,' she told the Manager on the phone. 'I have heard so much about them!'

The Manager preened herself. 'Oh, I think you'll find that Dreamydays is one of the finest facilities in the land,' she told the Mayor, and she said it again when the Mayor arrived for her visit.

Everything had been cleaned and polished, all the pink and blue bedspreads were ironed and exactly in place, and the old people were seated in neat rows round the walls of the lounge awaiting their special guest. Mrs Gusto spoke to each one and said how happy they must all be to live in such a fine facility. Most of them nodded and said nothing, not while the Manager was standing nearby.

But one old lady whispered that she didn't like bran biscuits *every* day. Mrs Chattery said, rather more loudly, that she didn't like being in the Blue Wing, she'd be happier in Pink. Mr Blunt complained again about the rows of orange marigolds in the garden. Then another old lady felt brave enough to say that she missed her Persian cat Fluffpot, and the old man beside her wished he could still keep racing pigeons.

The Manager raised her eyes to the ceiling and led the Mayor outside. 'They don't understand,' she said sweetly. 'We can't take risks with germs, and all my staff would leave if there were pets. It would be a nightmare!'

'Of course, I do understand,' replied Mrs Gusto, just as sweetly, thinking of her own menagerie at home. 'But we must remember that these old people have always had their own pets and gardens and they really miss them. And they've lived to a good old age alongside dogs and cats and parrots without catching any diseases so far, so they don't worry about germs.'

'But we haven't the staff to keep animals clean … you know, dealing with litter trays and fleas and all that sort of thing,' said the Manager, shuddering. 'And imagine the barking dogs … and the cat fights and the moulting feathers!'

'Oh, I'd rather not,' laughed Mrs Gusto, who had enough of them at home. 'Of *course* you can't turn the place into a zoo – the Health Department would close you down! But there might be other ways to make the old folk happier, to take their minds off the parrots and pigeons they can't have. Could we inspect the grounds?'

The Mayor saw what Mr Blunt meant about the straight lines of marigolds. They were boring, and smelly, too. The path was straight and it led nowhere except to the gate. The far corner of the grounds was bare and beyond the fence she noticed a large, empty block of land running downhill. 'What's beyond that fence?' she asked.

'It's council land, I believe,' said the Manager, 'reserved for possible future extensions to the Rest Home.'

'Indeed! And down the hill there, beyond the vacant land – those big trees, they must surely be the ones Mrs Chattery talks about? There don't seem to be any others.'

The Manager was puzzled; what had trees to do with the Rest Home? 'Trees? She hasn't mentioned them to me. She mostly talks about her parrot.'

'Mm, the famous Galahad,' smiled Gloria Gusto. 'Well, I'll be touch soon. You've given me some most interesting ideas, Manager. Thank you so much.'

As the mayoral car purred down to the Town Hall, Mrs Gusto rubbed her hands together and her head whirled with big ideas. Back in her office, she summoned the Town Planner, Gilbert Culvert, and asked him to bring the town map.

'There is a vacant block of land below the Rest Home,' she said. 'I saw it with my own eyes.'

The Town Planner found it on the map. 'Yes, here it is,' he said, poking it with his pen. 'It's council land, zoned for public use or for extensions to the Rest Home.'

'Indeed,' purred the Mayor. 'Now, can you show me where Mrs Chattery's place was, the one which was demolished for development?'

Gilbert Culvert turned faintly red, for he was still ashamed of some of the Burpwistle schemes. 'It would be about … here.' He jabbed at a spot in among the new streets. 'I remember because you've asked us to hold up the planning permit on that block. It's not far from the Rest Home and the vacant land. There used to be a creek running between them which has been enclosed in an underground drain.'

'Really? You mean there's a creek under all those buildings and streets?' gasped the Mayor.

'Oh, you can do wonderful things with concrete,' smiled Gilbert, dreamily.

Mrs Gusto kept the map in her office and when the Think Tank assembled again later in the week, she asked them to gather round it.

'Now, listen carefully, everyone. Here,' she pointed on the map, 'we have Dreamydays, and running down from it is this vacant block of council land, and just over here is Mrs Chattery's old block, still with its three gum trees. Mr Plank now owns it, but we have stopped him building on it for the moment. Any ideas?'

Mr Blunt couldn't wait. 'You bet! How can we get the Chatterswood land back from Plank? If it was joined on to the council land, there'd be a pretty decent open space there! Room for all sorts of things.'

'Indeed!' said Mrs Gusto. 'Now, remind me of all the things you talked about last week.'

'A skateboard park!' shouted Max.

'Somewhere for old legs to walk with things to look at,' said Mr Blunt.

'Nice trees with birds flying about, and seats,' was Mrs Chattery's wish.

'Places to go with my friends,' said Pippi.

'Somewhere to buy coffee or a sandwich,' suggested Lottie.

'Trails for walking, or prams and bikes,' said Aaron.

'And wheelchairs,' added Pippi.

As the ideas flew about, colliding with each other, a marvellous thing happened. Instead of people thinking only of their own needs, they began to realise that other people had different needs – that old people would want seats and shade, that wild birds would welcome nest boxes, that little kids would like a playground, that mums and dads would look for barbecues with shady trees, that bigger kids would like spaces to kick or whack balls, as well as the skateboard area, that teenagers would search for private nooks where they could talk by themselves, that dogs and cats should only be allowed on leashes if there were wild birds and animals.

'Right, let's start here, at Dreamydays,' said Mrs Gusto, pointing with her pen. 'If the fence to the vacant land was removed, a path could lead from the Rest Home into a park … a winding, smooth path, good for wheelchairs and stiff legs. Interesting plants and gorgeous shrubs along the way, not rows of marigolds.' She closed her eyes, while the Think Tank waited, spellbound.

'Don't forget seats,' squeaked Pippi, eyeing Mr Blunt's walking stick.

'Seats … yes, of course,' Mrs Gusto went on. 'Somewhere to sit … a sheltered spot …' Her eyes flew open. 'I know! A café along the path, all of your own, open on certain days, especially weekends. And I mean a real shop where you can spend money, not just a dreary canteen.'

'Really?' gasped Mrs Chattery. 'Just for us? So we could walk there and not have to go to town? We could take our visitors out for tea!'

Lottie suggested that the café could be run by a manager with volunteers to wait on tables. Mrs Gusto thought the council might employ a manager several afternoons a week.

Max began to fidget and then he burst out, 'But what about the skatepark?'

Mrs Gusto said, 'Don't worry Max, I haven't forgotten. Good planning takes a lot of time and thought you know.'

Aaron sighed. 'It also takes a heap of money,' he said. 'Who's going to pay for all this?'

For the first time, Mrs Gusto looked deflated. 'I'm not sure … yet.'

•••

Later, the Mayor called the Town Planner back to collect his map. They had another look at it. 'Supposing,' she said, 'just supposing that we could buy back Mrs Chattery's land from Plank, would it be possible to link it up with the council block? We are thinking about a bush park, with a playground and a special area for wheels … fast wheels of the scooter, rollerblade, skateboard, bike variety.'

Gilbert thought of his own four children. 'You mean a sort of wheelie place … for whizzing in … a Wheelie Whizzaground?' asked Gilbert Culvert, scratching his eyebrow. He was beginning to feel slightly excited.

Mrs Gusto let out a shriek. 'Gilbert! You've got it! Yes! A Wheelie Whizzaground – brilliant! And the old folk in their café up here on the slope might enjoy watching the youngsters whizzing – at a safe distance. If it had glass walls …'

'Café?' gaped Gilbert. 'You'd better tell me more …'

So Mrs Gusto told him some of the ideas that were floating around the Think Tank. 'If you planned it carefully, there could still be room for Rest Home extensions along the side. Gilbert, could you possibly draft some plans before the next council meeting?'

Gilbert Culvert, the Town Planner, stared. 'Who's going to pay for it all?' he asked.

'I don't know yet,' sighed Mrs Gusto. 'That's the trouble with big ideas.'

When Mayor Gusto put her proposals before the Blotsville council, they were flummoxed, but the Town Planner had drawn some delicious plans, showing trees and gardens and winding paths. The café overlooked a new park with an adventure playground and the Wheelie Whizzaground at the far end. There was a grassy open space for balls and tumbling and rushing about. On his plans he had drawn people enjoying themselves in all these places, especially whizzing.

He had asked his own kids and their friends to help him design the Whizzaground with all its swoops and curves and slopes and run-offs. Pippi and Max and two of Mrs Gusto's children were among them. They couldn't believe that planning was such fun and soon every kid in Blotsville knew about the scheme.

Near the adventure playground there were seats and a barbecue area among grass and trees. The council members licked their lips, it was so beautiful. They could imagine the old people sitting on the shady terrace outside the café, watching the birds flying by and the toddlers on the slides and the big kids zooming around the Wheelie Whizzaground in the distance. But, they wanted to know, where was all the money coming from?

'I'm not sure, yet,' said Mrs Gusto. 'We just need something or someone to give us a start. I am always optimistic – let us all hope that something will turn up.'

And it did.

•••••

Chapter 9

The O'Riley Gang - bank robbers

One morning, a little while later, a small paragraph appeared in *The Blotsville Bugle* reporting on a series of bank robberies in neighbouring suburbs. Nobody took much notice, for they could never imagine their own Blotsville Bank being held up, not while nice Mr Moon was the Manager.

The hold-ups were the work of the O'Riley Gang. Their leader, Wily O'Riley, was the brains behind the gang and he decided which bank to rob next. The gang's strongman was Luigi Lumpy, who was expert at clonking people with a baseball bat. He had very bulgy muscles but almost no brain. Their driver was Headlong Harry McSpurt. He always waited in the car outside the bank, with the engine running ready for the getaway dash, and his dream was to be a formula one grand prix champion. He hardly ever spoke except to growl, 'Vroom *vroom!*'

Wily O'Riley decided that the Blotsville Bank was next on the list. 'Heaps of dollars go into that bank from all those shops round the square,' he told his gang. 'I've been doin' my research. We'll go in termorrow, late arvo, when the customers have gone and the bank tellers are countin' up the day's money on their compooters. We'll take 'em by surprise!' he smirked. 'Should be a good haul!'

'Okay, boss,' growled Luigi Lumpy, stroking his baseball bat. 'Blotsville it is!'

'Vroom vroom vroom!' agreed Headlong Harry McSpurt.

Late the next afternoon after school, Pippi and Max were bringing Galahad and Sulf back from their outing in the square when a slinky black car oozled past and drew up opposite the bank. Two men got out, slipped stocking masks over their heads and grabbed a baseball bat each from the car. Another man stayed crouched at the wheel. There was hardly anybody in the street.

'Look!' hissed Pippi. 'Look at those men!'

Wily O'Riley and Luigi Lumpy were padding across the road on tiptoes, trying not to look like bank robbers.

'It's a hold-up! Here in Blotsville! Wow!' goggled Max. 'What'll we do? If we cross the road now we might get bashed!'

'Or taken hostage!' whispered Pippi. 'Stay behind the cypress trees until they go inside. Shut up, birds!' Hastily, she stuffed Sulf under her windcheater, so that he would think it was night-time, and Max did the same with Galahad. There were muffled squawks.

Wily stormed into the bank, shouting, 'This is a hold-up!' while Luigi Lumpy stayed at the entrance waving his bat and admiring Wily's performance through the doorway. The children seized the chance to dash across the road to Bitzers, with the two birds clutched tight under their windcheaters. They skidded up to their father at the counter.

'Quick, Mum! Dad! There's a hold-up!! At the bank – *do* something!'

Aaron stared. 'You're joking, ha ha!' he grinned. Hold-ups didn't happen in Blotsville.

'It's *true*! They've got baseball bats! And masks! Get the police!' hissed Pippi.

Aaron peered with one eye round the door, saw the black car with Headlong Harry McSpurt crouched at the wheel, and Luigi Lumpy's baseball bat waving about in the entrance to the bank.

'Cor!' gasped Aaron. 'You could be right! Lottie! Quick! Ring the police – the bank's being robbed. I'll fetch Douglas.' He strode towards the back of the shop and disappeared, while Lottie grabbed the phone and dialled the emergency number.

Pippi and Max squinted nervously into the street. They could just hear shouting from inside the bank, as Wily O'Riley roared at the tellers to fill his bag with banknotes. Luigi Lumpy was by now very jumpy and striding about in the entrance, twirling his bat and grinding his teeth.

Aaron returned from the back of the shop with a huge, slobbery German Shepherd straining on its leash. This was Douglas, who had once been a guard dog but was now retired because of arthritis. Aaron had decided to keep him to mind the shop. Douglas limped a bit, but he was very large, very well trained and deeply growly. He knew something was up – he could smell it.

The cockies were now sitting on the children's shoulders and wondering if they were meant to be awake or asleep, but when Douglas arrived Galahad let out a deafening shriek. Sulf got a fright and screamed, 'Quick march, quick march, *one two, one two*!! AT THE DOUBLE!!'

Hearing these orders screeched from next door, Luigi

Lumpy leapt down the steps from the bank, bounded across the road to the black car and piled into the front seat. 'At the *double!*' he yelled and Headlong Harry McSpurt slammed his foot down hard on the accelerator.

At that very moment, Sulf screamed '*Left wheel!*' and Galahad shouted '*Eyes right!*' Headlong Harry, who was not very bright, pulled the steering wheel hard to the left and looked out the window to the right and drove straight into a power pole, *zunk!* Harry clonked his nose on the steering wheel and blood spurted everywhere. Luigi, who hadn't had time to belt up, hit his head on the windscreen and fell back stunned.

The power pole wobbled and swayed, there were flashes and crackles, then all the lights and computers and cash registers and fans and electric jugs and freezers in the shops and offices went PHHHUT-T-T. People streamed out into the square, yelling 'What's *happened?* Is it an earthquake?'

Wily, waving a bagful of money and his bat, flew out of the bank to the black car. 'Wait for me, you *stoopid nuts!*' he bellowed, but just then Aaron and Douglas charged out from the pet shop.

'*Get 'im*, Douglas!' roared Aaron, letting go of the leash, and with huge, juicy snarls, Douglas leapt onto Wily, knocked him flat and sat on his head. The bag, gushing banknotes, skidded into the gutter. Pippi and Max rushed to grab it, gathered up the notes and handed the whole lot to the Bank Manager, Mr Moon, who was on all fours peering nervously round the door of the bank.

Just then the police van came squealing round the square on two wheels, its siren blaring. This was to be the easiest arrest the two policemen had ever had to make – Luigi was stunned, Headlong Harry was covered in blood and blubbering 'Vroom vroom vrooom', and Wily was half suffocated underneath Douglas's bottom.

After handcuffing the gang and locking them in the van, the police went into the bank to interview Mr Moon and his staff. But Mr Moon was unable to think of anything until he had finished counting the stolen money, and the tellers were so terrified and shaky that they could remember nothing either except Wily's baseball bat. All they wanted was a cup of strong tea, but they couldn't boil the water because the power was off. Two of them burst into tears.

'This is hopeless, they are all in shock!' growled the Police Sergeant. 'Maybe there were witnesses in the street.' He went outside, where a noisy crowd had gathered. 'Did anyone see what happened?' he shouted.

'Yeah, we did, we saw the car pull up,' said Max. 'We got Dad, he got Douglas, Mum called you, Galahad and Sulf

tricked two of them and Douglas caught the other one, and Pippi and I gave the money back to Mr Moon.' The Police Sergeant was rather confused by Max's statement, but he wrote it all down and tried to work it out while the prisoners were carried off in the police van to the lockup.

Several tow trucks zoomed up and blocked the road while their drivers argued about who would cart away the crumpled black car. The crowds and shopkeepers were getting very cross about the power blackout and the traffic jam. Another truck and a cherry picker arrived with men from the electrical company to fix the power pole. They began to herd the crowds out of the way. 'Come on, move it, or you'll all get electrocuted!' they yelled. In fact, everyone was yelling. The Blotsville square was in chaos.

'Huh, will you listen to 'em!' said Aaron, putting Douglas back on his leash. 'You'd think they'd be more

grateful. *We* just caught the O'Riley Gang!'

When the reporter and a photographer from *The Blotsville Bugle* arrived on the scene, however, they remembered the H. P. Burpwistle disaster and the clever cockies and they went straight to Bitzers. Max and Pippi told them the whole story and had their photographs taken, with Galahad, Sulf, Douglas, Aaron and Lottie.

Finally, a television camera crew arrived, wanting to film Galahad, Sulf and Douglas for the animal interest story on the nightly news.

'This'll be a winner!' cried the producer. 'Not just birds tricking the O'Riley Gang, but birds that can *talk*! Get 'em to say something on camera, kids!'

But no matter how much Pippi and Max and Lottie and Aaron coaxed and pleaded, Galahad and Sulf just sat and stared suspiciously at the big black eye of the TV camera, wondering what sort of a monster it was and if it was going to eat them.

'Go on, do that Hooray Hurrah Hooroo thing, *please*,' whispered Lottie into Galahad's ear, but Galahad just fluffed and flapped, while Sulf scratched his neck and flattened his crest.

'Blasted birds! I don't believe they can talk at all,' sighed the producer. 'We'll just have to film them sitting on your shoulders, kids, with the dog down in front.' So Douglas lay on the footpath and shut his eyes and yawned, while the birds perched on the children's shoulders, turned their backs on the big black camera eye and sulked. When the filming was over and the camera stowed away in the TV van, Galahad opened his mouth and croaked, 'Cats meat'.

•••••

Chapter 10

The bank offers a reward

Next morning, the Bank Manager, Mr Moon, read the report in *The Blotsville Bugle* over his breakfast muesli and muffins. It said:

O'RILEY GANG FOILED AT LAST!
POLICE POUNCE AT BLOTSVILLE!

Yesterday, the notorious O'Riley Gang were foiled and caught red-handed by a retired guard dog and two cockatoos from Bitzers, the well-known petorium in the Blotsville square. Not long ago, ex-Mayor Burpwistle threatened to close Bitzers' shop down as a health hazard. Last night Mr Burpwistle was not available for comment. The new Mayor, Ms G. Gusto, expressed her satisfaction at the capture of the gang by residents of Blotsville. 'This is a real feather in our caps!' she said.

'Look at this, dear,' said Mr Moon, reading the headlines to his wife. 'O'Riley Gang Foiled … Police Pounce at Blotsville!'

'What nonsense,' said Mrs Moon, buttering her muffin. 'There was no pouncing by the police. Those crooks were flattened before the police even got there. If

anyone pounced, it was that brave dog. Just you read on.'
Mrs Moon had read the paper from end to end before Mr
Moon had finished shaving.

Mr Moon's eyes opened wider as he read the report.
During the robbery, he had been so busy hiding behind
his big desk that he hadn't really seen what was going on
outside. 'You can't tell me,' he spluttered, 'that the
O'Riley Gang was foiled by an elderly dog and two
cockatoos. That's plain ridiculous. It makes no sense.'

'But that's what it says, dear,' munched Mrs Moon,
'and I daresay those two children had some part in the
pouncing, too – young Pippi and Max, who take those
two cockies for their outings. Are you going to offer them
a reward? What does head office say about it?'

'Reward?' Mr Moon dabbed his face with his napkin.
'I haven't had a chance to discuss such things with head
office,' he mumbled. 'I've been far too busy retrieving the
stolen money.'

'I thought those two kiddies did that,' said his wife,
'and anyway, I'm sure head office must be alarmed at
how much money the criminals nearly got away with –
how much was it again, dear?'

Mr Moon gulped, for that indeed was the first thing
head office had wanted to know. 'Seven hundred and
twenty-five thousand dollars in banknotes,' he told her.
His forehead broke out in a shiny sweat at the thought.
All those banknotes could have blown away or been
carried off by Wily O'Riley! 'It doesn't bear thinking
about!' he whispered.

'Oh, I think it does dear,' smiled Mrs Moon as she
gathered up the teacups. 'You really should think about it
and I'm sure you'll decide that the pounce was worth a

reward, a big one! Goodness me, almost three-quarters of a million nearly went down the drain!'

•••

Later that morning, Mr Moon walked along to Bitzers' Pet Shop. Galahad and Sulf were grooming themselves on their stands outside the door as Mr Moon entered the shop. He wasn't sure if he should wish them good morning and thank them for their part in the pounce, but in the end he just bowed slightly and Sulf croaked, 'Four dollars fifty – ping!' as he went by. Inside, Lottie was busily cleaning out the canary cages and Aaron was behind the counter.

'Mr and Mrs Bitzer, I've come to convey my thanks and that of the Blotsville Bank,' announced Mr Moon. 'Believe me, I had no idea of what was going on outside yesterday, for I was, er, trapped in my office while that O'Riley character was waving his club around and yelling at the teller. It was a nightmare!'

'You're lucky it wasn't a gun he was waving – we all were,' remarked Aaron, who was calmly filling bags with birdseed. 'My kids could have been shot!'

'Oh dear.' Mr Moon had been so busy counting the $725 000 that he hadn't thought of that. He had to mop his head again. 'But I now understand that the criminals were actually caught by *you*. How can I thank you enough?'

Aaron shook his head. 'No, no, no, not caught by *us*, actually – you oughta thank Galahad and Sulf and Douglas. And the kids. I just fetched Douglas and the wife called the police. No sweat.'

'Do you mean that the report in the *Bugle* was actually true? I find it hard to believe that the birds and the dog were responsible. It makes no sense.' Mr Moon sighed deeply. 'You know there was $725 000 in that bag and not a five dollar note was missing!'

'Go on, *that* much! Well, you can thank the kids for rescuing the money out of the gutter. It might have been swept down the drain if they hadn't grabbed it.' Aaron chuckled quietly. 'It could've ended up in the sea!'

Mr Moon turned pale again and sat on a stool beside the counter. 'Ah, so it could! In fact, my head office is offering a reward. That is what I've come to tell you. Head office would like to sponsor some community project or memorial as a mark of the bank's appreciation. We'd like you to suggest something suitable.'

'Go on!' remarked Aaron. 'Whaddya think, Lottie?'

'A community project?' she said. 'Ooh, that's nice. Something like a sculpture, you mean? Or a drinking fountain? We'll talk to the children after school – and let you know.'

•••

Max and Pippi were heroes at school for their part in the great pounce on the O'Riley Gang. The headmaster made a stirring speech at morning assembly. He said, 'Pippi and Max Bitzer have set a fine example by handing back all the money to Mr Moon and not slipping even *one* note into their pockets. They are a credit to the school and role models for you all!' and the whole school had hooted and stamped and later on called them the Rolymouldy Bitzer kids.

'What's a community project?' asked Max after school, when Aaron and Lottie had told the children about Mr Moon's offer of a reward.

'Well,' Aaron tried to explain, 'a community project is something that the town needs, like a new bus shelter, and the bank is offering to pay for it as a reward for catching the O'Riley Gang.'

'*A bus shelter?*' gaped Max. 'Bor-ing! We don't need a bus shelter!'

'You might,' said Aaron. 'But it was just an example. Have *you* got any ideas?'

'You know I have! We all have! A scooter track or a skatepark would be heaps better,' cried Max. 'You oughta ring up Mrs Gusto. What are you waiting for?'

Aaron scratched his head.

'This is excellent news, Aaron!' said Mayor Gusto, when Aaron rang to tell her about the Blotsville Bank's offer. 'This could be just the miracle we've been waiting for.' Gloria Gusto had known that something would turn up, but she wasn't expecting it to be a bank robbery. 'Now, we must strike while the iron is hot and before the bank goes cold on the idea. First I shall call a special meeting of the council and then I'll invite the Bank Manager to the Town Hall to discuss the bank's generous offer.'

'Let's hope it is generous,' sighed Aaron. 'I wouldn't bank on it.'

•••

The same feeling emerged from the special council meeting. 'You can bet the bank will sponsor the smallest thing it can find,' said one councillor gloomily.

'The plans should be made public quickly, then,' said another, 'saying how generous the bank is being … so that they won't want to back down and look mean!'

'Hear hear! You're right!' cried all the councillors, and they voted to make the plans public in *The Blotsville Bugle* straight away and to ask for suggestions and support.

•••

Next, Mrs Gusto invited the Bank Manager, Mr Moon, to visit her at the Town Hall.

'What a generous gesture your bank is making to the citizens of Blotsville,' she greeted him over a plate of scones. 'Mind you, the great Blotsville pounce on the O'Riley Gang *deserves* some memorial, and you must be very relieved that nobody was hurt and that you managed to retrieve such a large sum of money.'

'Quite so,' agreed Mr Moon, reaching for his mopping handkerchief. 'Has any decision yet been reached about the community project? My head office will be interested to know, as soon as possible.'

Mayor Gusto outlined the plan for Dreamydays and the new park and told Mr Moon that the plans would appear very soon in the newspaper. She ended by saying, 'It's early days yet, but I personally will suggest that the café be called the 'New Moon Café', if you are agreeable to that.'

'The New Moon … oh, yes, I like that,' said Mr Moon.

•••

The people of Blotsville eagerly supported the new plans, which appeared in colour in *The Blotsville Bugle*. The stallholders at the market organised a special fresh food festival and they made enough money in one day to pay for the adventure playground equipment. The most popular event was a competition for the best big hairy germ costume. The prize was a giant melon called the Burpwistle Trophy.

The Blotsville Concrete Company offered to donate concrete for the Wheelie Whizzaground, while two garden nurseries said they would supply twenty-five

small trees and fifty shrubs for the park. Bitzers' Pet Shop planned to donate nest boxes for the wild birds that would come to the trees.

Mrs Chattery rang the Town Hall. 'I want to put a plaque on my old goody gum tree in memory of Galahad's birthplace,' she said to the switchboard operator. 'That tree should never be chopped down, even though it's dead, for that is where cockies like to nest. Please tell the Mayor.'

The switchboard operator passed on these messages to the Mayor's office and added that she would be willing to form a Wednesday weeding squad to look after the gardens around the New Moon Café. 'Wednesday's my day off,' she explained, 'and I just love to get my hands dirty.'

The Manager at Dreamydays found a spare tea urn in a cupboard and donated it to the New Moon Café. She quite approved of a café, as it was far enough away not to interfere with the smooth running of the Rest Home. The District Nurse provided a large first aid kit, also to be kept at the café. 'You'll need this for the grazed knees and blood noses from the Whizzaground,' she said with a knowing look, 'and you'll probably find that some of the oldies will be expert at bandaging and mopping – just a bit out of practice.'

When he heard this, Aaron slowly had a brainwave. He said to Lottie, 'You know all those refugee animals that people bring here for us to look after?'

'I do,' said Lottie. 'They make a lot of extra work.'

Aaron pushed on. 'And you know how the oldies at Dreamydays are always wanting pets?'

'Yairs … and the Manager won't let them … well, what?'

'Well, it was Galahad and Sulf and Douglas who actually caught the O'Riley Gang, so the bank oughta commemorate that. They were the real heroes.'

'So …?' said Lottie, patiently.

'Well, near the café they could build an animal refuge – just for wild birds or animals that need looking after until they can go back to the bush. We could supply the food and stuff, and the oldies – the ones who wanted to – could look after them. Maybe some of the kids would like to help. Whaddya think, Lot?'

Lottie stroked his head. 'I think you're a clever old softie,' she said. 'A sort of Dreamydays Animal Annexe, but too far away for the germs to bother the Manager. Tell Mrs Gusto!'

Mayor Gusto was thrilled to find that support for the scheme was growing in so many interesting ways. 'But,' she said to the council, 'tea urns and weeding squads and orphan magpies are a long way down the track. We haven't even dealt with Mr Plank yet, or acquired Mrs Chattery's land. There's much to be done.'

•••

The bank's head office had finally agreed to pay for the New Moon Café building, provided that Mr Moon be invited to open it when it was finished. Over more plates of scones, Mrs Gusto also persuaded the bank to finance a small animal refuge nearby, to commemorate the clever birds and the brave dog who had outwitted the O'Riley Gang. And in honour of the two honest children who had rescued the bank's money, a flat corner of the park would be sponsored by the bank and developed as a special space for kicking, throwing and hitting balls and for running, jumping, handstands, chasey and other sorts of rushing about. This would be near the adventure playground which the market stallholders were to sponsor with the proceeds of their fresh food festival. Signs would be erected in all three places saying *Sponsored by the Blotsville Bank*.

An agreement was drawn up with the bank and in the small print at the bottom there was a clause that read:

The Bank will not be liable to supply any of the contents or equipment of the said café, animal refuge or playing field. Cups, saucers, spoons, coffee machines, urns, tables, chairs and any other furnishings; or cages, perches, water dishes, or food dishes; or balls, goal posts, etc., are not the responsibility of the Bank.

The councillors grumbled and muttered.

'Miserable skinflints,' said one.

'You'd think with all their millions they could donate a few spoons as well,' said another. But they had to agree to the bank's terms in case the bank got huffy and gave them nothing at all.

A Very Important Person from the bank's head office came to the Town Hall with Mr Moon to sign the agreement and, when the bank's cheque was safely in her hand, Mrs Gusto sighed and said to herself, 'Now we can call a special council meeting to discuss all the plans.'

But just before this happened, H. P. Burpwistle came back from the seaside.

•••••

Chapter 11

A park or a deathtrap?

H. P. Burpwistle was feeling much better after his rest cure in the fresh sea air. Copies of *The Blotsville Bugle* had been forwarded to him each week, so he had read all about the great pounce and the grand plan. He was very put out that he was no longer the Mayor during these important times. But H. P. Burpwistle was still a member of the town council, until the next election, even though he had been sacked as Mayor.

'I'm sick of sick leave,' he said to himself. 'It's time I went back to Blotsville before those councillors do something *stupid.*'

Nobody was at all pleased to see him back, but Mrs Gusto politely welcomed him to the special council meeting and hoped he was feeling better. She then went on to report on all the offers of help and donations that were pouring in – everything from truckloads of concrete to a first aid kit.

'The grand plan is within reach and getting grander every day!' she said. 'I think the council should now agree to pay for some of the extras like landscaping the parks. We should also discuss the possibility of buying back the adjoining Chatterswood land which Mr Plank has acquired, as it would be a wonderful addition to the park space.' Beaming, she then opened the meeting for discussion.

H. P. Burpwistle rose to his feet and a deep sigh passed round the table. 'I've been following events in Blotsville, never fear, despite my poor health,' he began, wagging his finger at them. 'Now, you all know my grave concerns for public health and safety. An animal refuge at the Rest Home would of course be a grave risk to the old folk, and a café so close to the cages would only make the danger of infection *worse*. However, there's an even more alarming item in the Mayor's report – that is the mention of a first aid kit in case of injuries to children in the play areas. Think of the risks!' he cried. 'Think of the concrete, bumpy tracks, roundabouts, skateboards, swings and slides, bicycles, searing hot barbecues … what use are a few bandaids and cotton wool for broken ankles, fractured skulls and third-degree burns, huh?' He thumped the table. 'The place will be a deathtrap!'

'But Mr Burpwistle, I thought you liked concrete!' said Mrs Gusto. 'And children have always played in places like that; they enjoy them and they learn to look after themselves.'

'Enjoyment has nothing to do with it,' huffed H. P. 'It will take only one parent to sue the council for a broken arm or a busted scooter, and soon they'll *all* be suing and then the council rates will have to go up to billy-o or we'll be bankrupt. That is why it is important to build six houses on the Chattery site – we'd get six more lots of council rates in the coffers.'

Mrs Gusto sank back, deflated. There was silence and then a low buzz of talk among her councillors. They all had stories of people demanding huge sums of money from doctors, schools, councils – people who decided to blame someone else for their accidents or bad luck or their own stupidity. Nobody wanted to side with H. P. Burpwistle, but they knew he had a point. New plans would probably have to be drawn, leaving out the risky bits and especially the Wheelie Whizzaground.

When the Town Planner arrived home after the meeting, he unrolled a copy of the beautiful plans that his kids had helped to draw. It was the best design he had ever worked on. He felt like crying, or tearing up the plans. Then he told the little Culverts the bad news and they did cry.

Very soon all the children in Blotsville had heard that their wonderful new park and Whizzaground were going to be much less wonderful.

'I *told* you,' stormed Max to no-one in particular. 'Why do grown-ups always have to ruin everything? Why do people have to *sue* people?'

Aaron tried to calm him down. 'I know, I know, it's not nice. But just occasionally it's okay for someone to sue – just think, if a zookeeper left the gate of the tiger's enclosure open by mistake, and the tiger walked out and chewed someone's leg off at the knee, and that person had to spend a long, expensive time in hospital and then couldn't walk properly ever again, and if that person had been a phys. ed. teacher or a police officer or a gardener and had to give up their job, then it would be quite okay to sue the zoo for being careless and causing all that suffering, see?'

Max frowned as he took all that in. 'Yeah, well, what about the others? Like the people who sue for a busted skateboard or an arm?'

'A lot of them are just greedy,' said Aaron. 'Look, if you fall off your skateboard and break your arm at the Whizzaground, it isn't really anyone's fault except perhaps your own. It's an accident, or you just aren't very good at skateboarding and you take a risk, but some people would try to blame the council who built the Whizzaground and say it isn't safe, because they think they can get some money out of it.'

Max was thinking hard. 'If I fell off my scooter and broke both legs in our backyard at home, could I sue you?' he asked. 'I wouldn't, but could I?'

'I dunno,' said Aaron. 'I s'pose you could try. You could say I'd left the dustbin in the wrong place and you'd fallen over it. But if you sued me and took me to court, it wouldn't do you much good, because I'd have to sell the house to raise the money to pay the lawyers and then you'd have nowhere to live and neither would we.'

'Yeah, that'd be dumb,' said Max, 'and I'd be pretty dumb not to see the dustbin.'

Max went to tell Pippi and his friends about suing.

•••

When the next issue of *The Blotsville Bugle* appeared, the front page featured a letter. It said:

Dear People of Blotsville,

We helped to plan a great Whizzaground with special things like the Wily Wheelie Roundabout and the Luigi Lumpy Bumpy Track and the McSpurt Vroom Vroom Home Straight. But now we probably can't have it because the council is afraid that someone might have an accident and sue them. That's because there are greedy people who think it's a great idea to blame someone else when it's probably their own fault or nobody's fault at all.

The best way to learn to ride a skateboard or rollerblades or a bike is in a proper Whizzaground, instead of on a footpath where you knock over old people or crash into brick walls or get run over. Kids are good about making up rules when they are playing, and the Whizzaground we planned was quite clever, with one-way tracks and grassy run-offs and a special place for beginners to practise. But it's all been spoilt now, because if just one person sues the council for some accident, then everyone else will start suing and the council will have to raise all its rates to pay the insurance companies.

We wish people wouldn't be so greedy and would learn to look after themselves better, and not spoil things for everyone else.

SIGNED (on behalf of Blotsville's kids): Pippi, Max, Billy, Tom, Tyler, Ravi, Stefano, Emily, Kim, Josie, Ben, Hans, Lulu, Pierre, Anil, Lucia.

PS: If people in Blotsville sue their own council and make the rates go up, it's like suing themselves because they are the ratepayers. That's really dumb.

•••

The Town Hall switchboard was jammed soon after the newspaper had been delivered and read in homes all over Blotsville. The switchboard woman had to call for assistance and the Mayor asked her to make a note of what callers said.

Older people said things like – 'When we were young, we were always falling out of trees and off our bikes and spraining ankles and jamming fingers in rat traps, but we didn't blame anyone else. We just learned to do things better next time. Kids have to learn the hard way.'

Mrs Chattery rang in and said, 'When Galahad was a baby, he fell out of his tree, but I looked after him and now he's a hero! It just goes to show.'

'What does it go to show?' asked the flustered switchboard woman, taking notes.

'That we should look after each other, silly!' retorted Mrs Chattery.

Younger parents felt sorry for the kids, but they all seemed worried to death about accidents and their kids hurting themselves, and about big medical bills and having to pay higher council rates. Life was one huge worry.

The whole of Blotsville was arguing. The Mayor and councillors spent sleepless nights and held emergency meetings. At every meeting H. P. Burpwistle smirked and said, 'I told you so. It's far too risky. We must drop the whole scheme, I tell you.' Whenever he said that, more and more of the other councillors nodded nervously.

Mayor Gusto was in despair. She was sick of Mr Burpwistle and his mean, miserable ways. She was sick of greedy people who thought of nothing but money and money-grubbing.

•••••

Chapter 12

You're nicked

The Mayor called an open council meeting about the park to which members of the public could come. The public gallery in the council chamber was packed. All the Bitzers were there, with Mr Blunt and Mrs Chattery, in the front row. The Manager of Dreamydays came along with several of the old people. There were children there with their parents, and market stallholders who had raised the money for the playground. There were newspaper reporters and shopkeepers and the manager of the Blotsville Concrete Company and the District Nurse and the Police Sergeant and Constable.

Mayor Gusto knew that this was her last chance. Somehow she had to convince the people of Blotsville and especially her council that this grand plan could work. H. P. Burpwistle stared at her meanly as she rose to her feet.

'People of Blotsville,' she said, 'the plans for our park are hanging in the balance. The Blotsville Bank and many of you have offered generous donations of money and time and materials. The children and the senior citizens have spoken out and they deserve to be heard. But more funds are needed to buy extra land and for landscaping, and unhappily there is much anxiety about the risks involved. We must now make a decision – we can't dither any longer. I just want to say this: let us all trust each other and seize the chance, let us build the children their Whizzaground and trust them to use it sensibly. Let us build the barbecues and the café and the playground and the animal refuge. For once let us think about people's happiness instead of about money. Let us all trust each other to support the project and make it work. *Let's do it*!'

There was a wave of cheering and stamping from the gallery. 'That's the way, Mrs G.!' roared Mr Blunt. 'Give it to 'em!'

Many of the councillors began applauding, but they wavered as H. P. Burpwistle rose to his feet. The cheers from above turned to hissing.

'Councils should *never* take risks!' he shouted above the din. 'Councils should proceed with caution. We don't want to rush into approving any building permits we might later regret. This project is full of risks – accidents, financial blow-outs, epidemics – you name it. Blotsville could be ruined! Bankrupted!'

The cheers fizzled out and Mrs Gusto could feel support slipping away from her. But suddenly someone upstairs stood up and roared, 'I wanna say something!'

The Mayor peered into the gallery and recognised the burly shape of Bentley Plank. 'Oh no! *Now* what?' she shuddered to herself.

Mr Plank was red-faced and sweaty and nothing would stop him. 'Let me tell you,' he boomed, waving his arm, 'that some of us *have* to take risks. Some of us can't wait forever for planning permits.'

Bentley Plank was in trouble, big trouble. Before H. P.

Burpwistle had messed up the car park plan, and been sacked as Mayor, Bentley Plank had bought up farm land, split it into tiny blocks and crammed lots of houses on it, then sold them quickly before the bank asked him to pay back his loan. But these days Plank found it impossible to get his shonky projects past the planning department, and the permit for Chatterswood had been stopped for some reason. Now the bank wanted their money, and Bentley Plank had begun to panic. He was drinking too much whisky and getting muddled, and right now he was wild with rage. All he wanted was to have his revenge on that fool, Burpwistle. Pointing a quivering finger at his cousin he bellowed, 'Burpwistle's bent! He's on the take! He oughta be in gaol.'

Pandemonium had broken out in the council chamber. 'What's Burpwistle done? Tell us!' shrieked the crowd.

'He's been taking bribes for years. Slipping things past council. Ask him who's paying him now, the rat!'

'Rat yourself!' yelled H. P. Burpwistle. 'You're the one who paid the bribes!'

There were angry shouts and boos. Mrs Gusto had given up calling for order and she sank back into her chair, crossing her fingers. With a bit of luck, she hoped, Plank and Burpwistle would destroy each other and both of them might end up in gaol.

Plank's next bombshell caused a sensation. 'Yeah!' he bellowed at Burpwistle. 'And who took $1000 to have Mrs Chattery's dump condemned? Eh? Six lovely new houses I was goin' to build there, until you got yourself sacked, you moron! And those blasted gum trees are still there! Yer can't build anything with them there. Yer can have the rotten place back, for all I care!' he muttered. 'I'm sick of it! I got it for a song – that old witch-woman didn't have a clue – so you can have it for yer park, ha ha ha!' He was half crazy with rage and frustration and whisky.

'I am not a witch-woman!' Mrs Chattery gasped, waving her umbrella at him. 'I always knew you were crooked, you ... you dreadful man! Bent by name and bent by nature, that's you!' she cried. 'And now Burpwistle, too! Blots on the landscape, both of you! I was right to call this place Blotsville.'

This took a moment to sink in, then someone called out, '*You* called it that? What about our illustrious pioneer Blot?'

'I *told* you I'd never heard of him,' Mrs Chattery retaliated. 'Why doesn't anyone listen? Anyway, if my land and the goody gum trees can be part of the park, I'll die happy!'

Mayor Gusto's head was spinning. Too much was happening all at once – how ever could she restore order? But the shouting died and her problem was solved as the Police Sergeant strode to the front.

'Serious allegations have been made by Messrs Plank and Burpwistle against each other,' he pronounced in his official voice. 'Can anyone confirm these allegations?'

After a hushed pause, Gilbert Culvert, the Town Planner, rose nervously to his feet. 'Well, S-sergeant,' he stammered, 'there's been a nasty smell in planning and building matters for some time, and shortly before Mr Burpwistle was ... um ... removed from office as Mayor, I overheard Mr Plank offering him m-money for the new car park job on the market site.' Now that he had started, Gilbert Culvert began to feel happier than he'd felt in a long time. 'They were in the passage and my office door was ajar, which shows how careless they'd become. Through the crack I saw Mr Plank slip Mr Burpwistle an envelope and tell him to put it towards that s-speedboat he'd always wanted.'

A ripple of 'O-o-oohs' and 'A *speed*boat!' ran round the room.

'I see!' said the Sergeant. 'And would you be ready to testify to this in court, Mr Culvert?'

'Yes, I would,' said Gilbert, stoutly. 'Those plans of Plank's were a disgrace. He knew nothing about good planning and cared less. I wish I'd blown the whistle sooner, but I was scared of losing my job – I've got four kids to feed. But I hated what was happening, I can tell you.' He sat down, gasping. Then he stood up again. 'Oh … and take it from me … the plan for the new park is the best thing I've ever done. It's a ripper!'

Amid more cheers, the Police Sergeant signalled to his Constable, who had climbed up to the gallery to stand behind Plank. 'Right!' announced the Sergeant sternly. 'H. P. Burpwistle and B. Plank, I am arresting you both. You're nicked! You will now be taken to the station to be charged on suspicion of bribery, corruption and shady deals.'

The police snapped handcuffs on the two prisoners, seized them by their collars and marched them out of the hall amid uproar. Gilbert Culvert was mobbed and nearly knocked over by hearty pats on the back.

'I think we've won,' said Bertie Blunt to Abigail Chattery. '*We* started all this, you know, with the Better Blotsville Brigade. Shows what oldies can do if they try!'

'Wow!' shouted Max. 'That was just like on telly!'

Mayor Gusto was speechless.

•••

And so Blotsville got its park. It became the best park in the whole region and wheelie championships were held at the

Whizzaground twice a year. The Blotsville Vroom Vroom team nearly always won. The first aid box at the New Moon Café was ready if grazed knees or blood noses needed attention, and the old people turned out to be expert bandagers, as the District Nurse had known they would.

The old creek was rescued from its drain and turned into a wetland for waterbirds and frogs and pond life. A plaque was placed on Mrs Chattery's dead gum tree, saying 'Birthplace of Galahad, Blotsville's Beloved Galah'. Nearby, a very large bird feeder table was built and named 'Cockies' Café', with another plaque saying 'In honour of Sulf, Blotsville's Champion Cockatoo.'

Aaron made weekly trips to the wild animal refuge behind the New Moon Café with supplies of birdseed and food. Banks of trees and gorgeous shrubs were planted and the wild birds began to return to Blotsville. When the trees grew tall enough, Aaron installed nest boxes so the birds could breed.

Max and Pippi and their friends sometimes came to help the old people clean out the refuge or to set free any of the creatures who had recovered from their broken wings or squashed toes.

On fine days, when the old people sat on the terrace at the New Moon Café, Aaron would take Douglas to visit them, and the old dog hobbled round among the chairs and tables being stroked. On such fine days, Aaron also took Galahad and Sulf with him in the van, with special perches for them to sit on in the courtyard while they talked to Mrs Chattery and Mr Blunt and all the other old people. No birds or animals were allowed into the Café, in case of germs.

Soon after the New Moon Café had opened for business,

the Manager took a visiting aged care expert from North America to inspect it and to see how the old people at Dreamydays spent their time. It was one of Aaron's visiting days, too, and they arrived at the courtyard to find Galahad and Sulf on their stands, flapping and shrieking, while Douglas was happily wandering about eating bits of cake. The old people and the cockies were having crazy conversations and there was a jumble of shouts and laughs and exclamations and strange noises, like this:

'Who wants a scone? … Pink jam please … Who's a pretty boy, then? … Blot blot blotface! … You twerp! … Muffins for me … Flap flap flap … Thank goodness for feathers ha ha ha! … Eyes right! … Screech … Weak black tea thank you … O joy and rapture! … *Woof woof* … Pass the sugar dearie … Cats meat cats meat! … Shriek … Blot on the landscape! … At the double, one two one two … Woof woof … Four dollars fifty – ping!'

The Manager was appalled. How had she ever allowed this to happen? The expert stood gaping, bewildered by the scene before her, but at last she whispered to the Manager, 'Say, they're all *laughing*. They're having *fun* – it's great, it's unreal! How *do* you do it, huh? What's the secret?'

Before the Manager could think of an answer, the whole group of croaky and screechy voices suddenly joined in the chorus of:

Hoo-ray, hoo-rah for the ga-la-la!

Hoo-roo for the cock-a-too!

And Mr Blunt called out, 'G'day Manager! Bring your mate over and have a cuppa!'

•••••

Epilogue – parrot paradise

As time passed, Galahad and Sulf flapped their big lopsided wings more and more often and stretched up longingly from their perches and chains towards the trees and the wide, windy sky.

Pippi said to Aaron one day, 'It's not fair – their wing feathers are nearly grown back, so instead of clipping them again couldn't we let them have a fly round? Do you think they'd come back?'

'I dunno,' frowned Aaron. 'Anyway, you'd have to ask Mrs Chattery and Mr Blunt – they own them.'

The two old people didn't know whether the birds would come back, either, and they looked anxious. Then Max said, 'But where else would they go? The best place for birds in Blotsville is this park, isn't it! It's parrot paradise!'

And Mrs Chattery said, 'I do believe you're right, young Max. And it doesn't seem fair that we can enjoy the park and they can't, after all they did to catch those Wileys and Lumpys.'

'Righto,' agreed Bertie Blunt. 'Let's take the risk.

That's what the Mayor told us to do and it's worked a treat so far. Let's do it!'

So, one day, when their wing feathers had completely grown again, Galahad and Sulf were let off their chains outside the New Moon Café. Many of the old people from Dreamydays came to watch and even the Manager turned up. The school arranged a special excursion for the children as part of their science lesson. Aaron and Lottie closed the shop and went too.

Mrs Chattery and Mr Blunt were asked to undo the chains.

'Off you go, dearies,' sniffed Mrs Chattery, who had her pink handkerchief ready. She gave Galahad a parting stroke and kissed his head.

At first nothing happened. Galahad sidled along his perch and Sulf flapped a bit. 'Come on Sulf, quick march! One two one two!' urged Mr Blunt.

'They won't be able to fly, y'know,' said Aaron, 'because they never have. They'll have to learn how and build up their flying muscles.'

Both birds began flapping hard. Then Galahad jumped off his perch and fell onto the ground. It was all very disappointing. Sulf aimed for a nearby bush and missed it by a metre. It was quite embarrassing, really.

Lottie had tears in her eyes. 'Oh, dear, I don't think we should watch. Will they ever learn to do it?'

'Course they will,' said Aaron, 'but it'll take time, like learning to ride a bike, or a skateboard. If they flap and practise a lot, they'll get the hang of it. I'll bring 'em up here each day for a training session.'

And gradually they did get the hang of it. One day, Galahad flew as far as the nearest small tree, and the next

day Sulf, who was heavier, did the same. And over another week they managed to fly a bit higher and further until, one day, they both flew right over the park and landed rather clumsily in Mrs Chattery's dead gum tree, where they bobbed up and down and shrieked and sharpened their beaks on the branch.

The onlookers held their breath. Would they fly away for ever? Mrs Chattery was clutching her pink handkerchief to her cheek. Mr Blunt gripped his stick until his knuckles were white. Max and Pippi felt sick. Even the Manager held her breath.

Then Lottie filled a dish with sunflower seeds, rattled it round a bit and placed it on the bird feeder. Galahad and Sulf cocked their heads and flapped, then swooped back to the seed dish and their friends.

'They're going to stay!' Everyone relaxed. Some cried and some laughed.

'Oh, goody goody Galahad!' wept Mrs Chattery.

'And dear old Sulf,' sniffed Mr Blunt. 'Good chaps!'

When they had crunched all the seeds, Sulf and Galahad flapped their big strong wings for a while, had a drink of water, and then took off with a whoosh. They soared back to the gum tree and sat on the branch which had been Galahad's birthplace, and the people of Blotsville below heard a familiar duet floating down from on high:

Hoo-ray, hoo-rah for the ga-la-lah!
Hoo-roo for the cock-a-too!

Other books by Mary Steele, published by Hyland House:

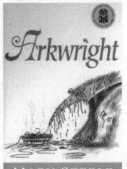

Arkwright
CBCA Book of the Year for younger readers (1986)
ISBN 1 875657 24 X
Also available: **Citizen Arkwright**
ISBN 1 875657 25 8

A Bit of a Hitch and Other Stories
CBCA short-listed book (1996)
ISBN 1 875657 58 4

Tenterhooks
ISBN 1 86447 015 1

BACK IN PRINT
Featherbys
CBCA short-listed book (1994)
ISBN 1 875657 05 3